in the
middle

CARIN FAHR SHULUSKY

In the Middle
Carin Fahr Shulusky
Fossil Creek Press

Published by Fossil Creek Press, St. Louis, MO
Copyright ©2021 Carin Fahr Shulusky
All rights reserved.

Editors: Carol Corley, Christine Shulusky Blonn, Kristi Berner, and Kay Clark-Uhles

Cover illustrator: Janice Schoultz Mudde

Cover and Interior design: Davis Creative, DavisCreative.com

Publisher's Cataloging-In-Publication Data
(Prepared by The Donohue Group, Inc.)

Names: Shulusky, Carin Fahr, author.

Title: In the middle / Carin Fahr Shulusky.

Description: St. Louis, MO : Fossil Creek Press, [2021]

Identifiers: ISBN 9781736241707 (paperback) | ISBN 9781736241714 (ebook)

Subjects: LCSH: Advertising executives--Fiction. | Adult children of aging parents--Fiction. | Aging parents--Care--Fiction. | Brothers and sisters--Fiction. | Mothers and daughters--Fiction. | LCGFT: Domestic fiction. | BISAC: FICTION / Family Life / Siblings. | FICTION / Family Life / General. | FICTION / Christian / General.

Classification: LCC PS3619.H855 I5 2021 (print) | LCC PS3619.H855 (ebook) | DDC 813/.6--dc23

2021

This book is dedicated to
Dorothy Hoehne Fahr, my mother,
the source of my inspiration and
creativity and all that I am.

Acknowledgments

I'd like to acknowledge my two terrific editors: my dear friend Carol Corley and my brilliant daughter, Christine Shulusky Blonn. I'd also like to acknowledge my husband Richard, who was always there for me and my son Andy, who always brings laughter.

I'd also like to acknowledge my three siblings, Mary Bellrose, Linda Bickford and Larry Fahr, always a part of me, and my ever enthusiastic brother-in-law, Geoff Gloak, his wife Kristi and their daughter Gemma.

Table of Contents

A Time for Everything

There is a time for everything,

And a season for every activity under heaven:

A time to be born and a time to die,

A time to plant and a time to uproot,

A time to kill and a time to heal,

A time to tear down and a time to build,

A time to weep and a time to laugh,

A time to mourn and a time to dance,

A time to scatter stones and a time to gather them,

A time to embrace and time to refrain,

A time to search and a time to give up,

A time to keep and a time to throw away,

A time tear and a time to mend,

A time to be silent and a time to speak,

A time to love and a time hate,

A time for war and time for peace.

Ecclesiastes 3:1-8 (NIV)

Chapter 1

The Call

It was a normal fall day. Pretty much like any other day. The sky was blue and the sun was setting on the brilliant red trees as I walked into my house after a long day at work. I had just taken off my coat when the phone rang. It was one of those calls you've always feared but hoped would never come.

"Mom is in the hospital. We don't know exactly what's wrong but fear it might be her heart," said my sister, Maria. She was the oldest and had been *in charge* my whole life. "How fast can you get here?"

"I can be there in 15 minutes," I told her putting my coat back on. As I climbed back in my car I quickly called my husband, Geoff and left him a message. Geoff was my husband of twenty-five years. He worked in a bank and was always hard to track down. The only thing that mattered now was getting to the hospital as fast as possible. My hands were shaking as I started the car. A few tears crept down my face.

It's not like this was a surprise. Or was it? Mom was eighty-two—but she was Mom. She was supposed to live forever. She struggled to walk, but insisted on doing everything herself. She would never consider living with me or one of my two siblings. She had run the show since Dad died over thirty years ago. Even in her diminished state, she was always the one we turned to for everything. Mom knew all the important things in life: Why the baby's crying; is this a cold or something worse? Why did the cake fall? How do you cook a turkey? What's wrong with the fridge? plumbing? When should you plant tomatoes? corn? She was a better weather predictor than any weatherman. She always knew when it would snow, rain, or storm. Sure, she was struggling hard the last few months, but she was Mom.

I was the middle child. Mom relied a lot on Maria, the oldest, and John, *the* son, who was the youngest. But I was never that close to Mom. Did I miss my chance? My life was busy with work, two kids, a house, and a husband. I didn't spend a lot of time with Mom, mostly just holidays and birthdays. We celebrated everything, from Fourth of July to Ground Hog's Day. Every special day called for loads of food, piles of dessert, and tons of dirty dishes. We couldn't celebrate without everyone being there, eating 'til they burst.

Holidays were crazy busy with decorating, cooking, setting tables, and cleaning up afterwards. There never seemed to be time to just talk. Not that we were good talkers anyway. Mom's way of dealing with everything in life, from the small setbacks to major events, even Dad's death, was "Let's not talk about it. It will just make us sad." So, we move on and on and on.

I thought the hospital was close, but this drive was taking forever. We live in a suburb of St. Louis. Traffic is not usually a problem. Where did all this traffic come from? Questions flooded my thoughts. Should I call the kids? What would I say? I would wait until I knew more. My mind was flashing with scenes from the past. Mom was always there at every important event. She was there when the kids were born and baptized, for every one of their birthdays, when I got married. She gave us everything she had. She was there for parent's day at college. She drove two hours and could only stay long enough to have lunch, but she was there. When I graduated from anything or got an award, she was there. Now she needed me and I had to get to that hospital.

Finally, it came in sight. I raced to emergency. Surely, she was still in emergency.

"Do you have Dorothy Schmidt here?" I asked.

"Who are you?" I was asked.

"I'm Carrie Young, her daughter," I told her impatiently.

"You'll have to wait" was the harried response. An agonizing ten minutes later, I was told she was in a room on the fifth floor. How did that happen so fast? Wasn't she just rushed to the hospital? As I approached Mom's room, I saw Maria and John in the hall, deep in conversation.

"So, how's Mom? What does the doctor say? How did she get to a room so fast?" Questions poured out of my mouth.

Maria answered, "Well, we've been here for about five hours. Don't look so shocked. You were at work, and we thought there was no need to tell you until we knew more."

I gave an exasperated glance at John, but he just shrugged, as if to say, *Maria's in charge. What can I do?* Such is our family dynamic. No point in trying to change it now.

"The doctor said he thinks Mom has a severe case of congestive heart failure," Maria continued, ignoring my look. "It means that fluid is collected around her heart and that's why she has been so exhausted and had trouble breathing," she continued before I could ask the questions. "People live with congestive heart failure; but the thing is, there was probably some event that caused this to happen, like a minor stroke or heart episode that weakened her heart. So, the bigger question is: Will that happen again?"

Now I was scared. Stroke. Heart attack. This was all pretty scary stuff. Then it happened. The thing I was working so hard at avoiding. A tear started to swell in my eye, then another, then a flood.

Maria saw it coming and her eyes swelled too. "We can't do this now," she said. "Let's wait for more information. Do you want to go in and see her?"

Why couldn't I be the strong one, the one who doesn't cry at the drop of a hat? Did she have to get all the best character traits?

"Okay" I mumbled.

"No tears now," Maria warned. "We don't want to worry her."

Worry her? I thought. What about me? I'm terrified. How do I do this?

I've never been good at hiding my feelings. This is going to be tough. Now was my time to show some grit. This is not a Lifetime movie. This is life.

Bravely, I entered the room. "Hi, Mom. How are you doing?" I asked. Boy, that was brilliant!

"Well," she answered, "I am in the hospital. I hate this bed. It's terribly uncomfortable. They don't come when I press the buzzer. I want to go home. But other than that, I guess I'm okay."

That's my mom. She has completely missed the obvious. She *is* seriously ill. But that's not the issue in her mind. It's the details that count, and it's all about how soon she will be home.

"Well, Mom, you are in the hospital. It's not going to be like home, but I think you will have to be here awhile."

"I don't understand why," she argued. "I'm not sick. I'm just tired all the time and I can't breathe well."

What can I say? That, of course, is the very definition of "very sick," but I can't tell her that. I'm not sure I could explain it so she would understand anyway. I certainly don't want to say what I'm thinking. I'm scared for her, but don't want to scare her.

"Well, Mom, I think the doctors need to figure out why you're so tired. It could mean something. They need to get the fluid out from around your heart, too, so you will feel better. Then you can go home."

This was the best I could do. I knew I couldn't continue this conversation without giving away my fears or information we weren't ready to share with her. I had to come up with another topic.

"The last time I was in this hospital was when Grandma had hip surgery," mom said.

I was hoping she remembered the good surgery, not the hospital stay before her death.

4

"I do remember that," she said. "She didn't like this place either. Did you know she never went to the hospital until she was seventy-five years old?"

Now she was reminiscing about Grandma. That's a good distraction, I thought. Let's go with that.

"You mean she never went to the hospital to give birth to any of her six babies?" I asked even though I knew the answer. It seemed like a safe subject. Maybe it would take her mind off the uncomfortable part of the hospital.

"She had all six of us right at home. Did I ever tell you that she always called me her 'bargain baby'? The doctor didn't arrive until after I was born so he only charged half price. That always made her smile."

"I can't imagine having a baby at home."

There was so much about my grandmother and Mom's early years I didn't know. Maybe this was the time to learn. Perhaps it wasn't too late.

"She never complained about giving birth at home. It was natural then."

"Was there anything Grandma did complain about?" I suddenly wanted to know everything about my mom and grandma. After all, this was my history too.

"She often talked about the worst day of her life. It was my earliest memory. I could never get this day out of my head," Mom reminisced.

"Tell me about it. What happened?" I asked. Now I was forgetting the hospital too.

"It was the beginning of the Depression, although we didn't know it yet. I was maybe four. Uncle Fred was five, I was four, and Martha was three. Robert was just a baby. We lived in a dingy little shack. Grandpa had saved enough for a new house. Grandma was so excited about the new house. She hated that little shack. It must have been an awful place to have four little babies. There was no running water. She pumped water from a well to bathe the babies. I remember it was a very dark place, freezing cold in winter, burning hot in summer. But this day was

5

going to be our last in this dismal place. We had a new house, with glass windows and a real sink with running water.

"Grandma and Grandpa loaded everything we had and all of us in the old farm wagon. There we sat with every worldly possession we owned—which wasn't really all that much—piled on top of that rickety old wagon. It was pulled by our two plow horses, Bessie and Sally. They weren't in much better shape than the wagon. The only thing left to do was to drive up to the bank and get the money they had carefully saved for five years and we could have our new house. They never spent one dime on any frivolity, like sugar or candy or fruit. It all went into that bank and their dream of a better home.

"We pulled up to the bank and immediately knew something was terribly wrong. There was a mob of people around the bank making a lot of noise. Grandma handed me the baby and told us to stay put while she and Grandpa went to find out what was going on. It seemed like an eternity before they returned.

"I knew it was bad news. Grandma's face was red and puffy. I believe, in my whole life, that's the only time I ever saw her cry. Maybe that day she cried it all out. You see, the bank had closed the day before. There was a run on the bank, and they didn't have enough to give everybody their money so they simply closed. The bank owners left town before anybody knew what had happened and all our money was gone, every last cent."

"What did you do about the new house?" I asked in astonishment. Could this be true? How horrible!

"I never saw that new house again," she said sadly. "I guess some other family bought it. All I knew was that we carried all our stuff back into that tiny, dark, cold house. Not one word was said by anybody. In fact, Grandma didn't say a word for days. She just sat in the corner, holding the baby."

"But you did move eventually, didn't you?"

"We lived in that ugly house another ten years. Then my grandfather sold Grandpa the land where they lived when you were little. Grandpa and his brother had built that house, with a little help from some neighbors. It wasn't as big as you knew it, at first. They added on a couple of times. But it was so much better. It felt like a castle to us. I don't think we got too excited before we moved. We never trusted that it would happen. We spent all our hope and excitement for the house we lost. In many ways, Grandma never quite got over that. I think she mourned her lost house the rest of her life."

What could I say? Such a sad story.

Mom was all talked out and shortly fell asleep. I sat watching her sleep, so old and frail. Is this the same young mother who cradled me when I was little? Is this the caring Mom who mopped my brow when I was delirious with fever? Was this the widow who drove four hours to spend one hour with me in college? Was she the middle-aged woman who worked all day to keep our business alive and scrubbed the floor at night and put up the Christmas tree before dawn? How much had she suffered for me? I never really appreciated all she did for me, for us all.

I knew at this moment that I would make it my mission to find out all I could about this wonderful woman, the woman who gave everything for her family. She had so much history that I never made an effort to discover. I was not going to let her leave me without learning her story. I was not going to let her go without showing her how much I appreciated all she had done.

Chapter 2
A Diagnosis

Maria insisted that one of us stay with Mom around the clock. I managed to convince her that Mom would mostly be sleeping during the night, so she agreed to the six a.m. to ten p.m. watch. But Maria did have a good point, as she always did. If the doctor came and talked with Mom, we'd never know what he said. Mom's ability to repeat a conversation was mostly nonexistent. Sometimes she was completely cogent and other times she made no sense at all. She didn't like sharing personal information anyway; so, you can be certain, if the doctor said anything embarrassing, which was just about anything to do with bodily functions, she'd never repeat it. We weren't quite sure how well she could describe what had been going on with her in the last few weeks, either. Maria was right. One of us had to be there when the doctor came. And that could be anytime.

This was going to be hard. I had work, a desk full of papers, clients to visit, projects to supervise. I couldn't just disappear for a day.

I took the early watch. Getting up early was always easy for me and then I could just miss a few hours of work. It seemed like a good plan. Maria and John both worked on the family farm. Their days were long and hard but more flexible than mine, at least I thought so.

I worked for Ryan Advertising. My boss, Matt Ryan, never missed work for anything. Even when his wife had cancer, he made it nearly every day. Not that it was a good idea—she struggled terribly—but work came first. She knew that, I knew that, we all got it. I didn't know how

I was going to explain this to him. In order to understand love, you first had to have a heart. Maybe that's a little harsh. Maybe it's not. I suppose that's why I've always called him, Mr. Ryan and not Matt. He's an old fashion man and just seems more like a Mr. than a Matt.

So up I got at 4:45 the next morning. It had been a rather long night. There were lots of calls to make. My daughter Julie was in college, and we had a very long talk about Grandma. My son, Adam, was in high school and had basketball practice until ten p.m., so I had to wait for him to get home to tell him about Grandma. He's the stoic type but was still concerned. I talked to two of Maria's children because they wanted another perspective. I talked to Mom's siblings, Uncle Fred and Aunt Martha, and best friend, Joan. They all wanted way more detail than I could tell, particularly after telling it so many times. By the time I dragged myself to bed, it was hours past my bedtime.

I walked into the hospital right on time. As I entered Mom's room, I saw the doctor sitting at the side of her bed talking to her. Don't these doctors ever sleep? Ten more minutes and I would have missed him. Maria would have never let me forget it.

I rushed to the bedside. "Good morning."

"Do you know this lady?" the doctor said to Mom.

"I guess so," said Mom. "I gave birth to her."

Funny!

"I'm Carrie, I'm her daughter." I told the doctor.

"Well, I'm glad you're here. That's okay, Dorothy, isn't it?" He asked as I shuddered.

What if she said no? What would I do then? I quietly prayed, *Please, dear God, let her say yes.*

"Oh, I guess so," Mom replied.

Thank you, God!

"I'm Dr. Schultz, a cardiologist. The hospital assigned me to your mother's case," said the doctor. "I'm going to ask some questions. Can you tell me, Dorothy, when you first started feeling bad?"

"Well," Mom said, "it was about two weeks ago. I was in my basement. I had just returned from feeding the chickens. Nobody ever gives them shells. That makes the eggs stronger you know. Anyway, I was about to go up the stairs, and all of a sudden everything went dark. My ears were pounding, my arm hurt like crazy, I couldn't see, and I fell to the floor."

I must have looked like I was just sucker punched. I'm hearing my mom talk of a heart attack that she told no one about. Why didn't she mention this before? Did Maria know and not tell me. How could this happen?

"I can tell from your expression," said Dr. Schultz, "that this is the first you've heard of this episode."

"Yes, we didn't know," I stuttered.

"Mom, why didn't you tell us?"

"Well, I lay on the floor for a while and thought, This is where I'm going to die, right there in the basement."

"But, Mom," I almost shouted, "there's a phone down there. Why didn't you call 911?"

"I didn't want to trouble anyone," she said seriously. "Anyway, what could they do? They'd just haul me off to the hospital in one of those ambulances. And they never find anything."

Unbelievable!

"Oh, I think they would have found something this time," I nearly shouted.

How on earth can we help her when she doesn't even let us know she had a heart attack?

Dr. Schultz saw my exasperation and held up his hand, with a smile.

I understood. It was no time for incrimination. We needed to find out how to help her.

"So, what happened next?" he asked.

"Well, I laid there for, oh, I don't know, maybe an hour. The floor was cold. Slowly, I got my eyesight back, and my head and arm didn't hurt so much. So, I crawled up the stairs, pulling myself along the banister, and went to bed. The next day, I didn't feel like getting up at all. I stayed in bed a couple of days and then went back to my normal routine around the farm, only I just couldn't do what I usually did."

Of course, you couldn't, I thought. You had a heart attack! I couldn't say all I was feeling. It wouldn't help anyway.

"We thought you had the flu," I said weakly. The doctor must think we are terrible children. I bet he thinks we don't care at all about our mother. How do I tell him that's not the truth? Or is it? Maybe we should have been more attentive.

I had talked with Maria several times in the last two weeks about Mom not feeling well. We both thought it was just a case of the flu. How could we have known? How would we know the next time if she doesn't tell us? She has always been so stubbornly independent. She never asks for help, but this is different. This is life-threatening.

"Well," said Dr. Schultz, "my guess is you had some kind of a heart episode. But since it's been two weeks since the event, our tests won't show very much. What we do know is that the event weakened your heart and it wasn't pumping properly, allowing for fluid to collect around the heart. That is congestive heart failure."

"So, what's the cure?" I asked.

"There really is no cure," he replied. "Once the heart is damaged, you can't reverse the damage."

"What is the treatment? Surely, there is something you can do?" I asked.

"We put your mom on intravenous diuretics last night and got six pounds of fluid from her heart," Dr. Schultz said. "That's a start. We'll continue this treatment. Long term, the treatment is medications to thin the blood and keep it moving. Your mom should try to eliminate salt from her diet, as much as possible, and monitor her weight carefully. I'd suggest she be weighed every morning. If there is any sudden weight change, you should call us right away. I'm going to order some tests. Will you be around for a while to sign some papers?" he asked me.

"Sure, I'll be here as long as you need me," I replied and took a seat next to Mom.

"You don't need to stay with me," Mom said. "I'll be just fine. It's nothing really. I don't want you to get in trouble at work."

Mom never understood what I do. I'm in advertising. Not the big TV stuff, more local businesses. I'm an account executive. I don't even create anything. Mostly, she doesn't understand anything that doesn't involve growing things, planting, harvesting, and plucking. I can't explain why it's so important to be at work. It's not like the earth will stop spinning if I don't show up, but I could lose my job and that would be the end of the world for me.

"It's okay, Mom. I'll just stay until these tests are over. I'm going to call my office first."

I stepped into the hall and called Maria and told her what had occurred this morning with the doctor. She was as much in shock as I was. She was stuck finishing some work at the farm and couldn't leave. I told her I'd stay. Then I made the call to my office.

It didn't go quite as badly as I expected. Mr. Ryan was understanding, sort of. He said not to worry, he'd cover with my clients and make sure all the deadlines are met. I had to wonder if that meant he would take over my clients or reassign them. His fake concern was even more scary than screaming at me. But I had to stay. For once in her life, Mom needed me. Not Maria. Not John. She needed me.

I went back in the room. "We've got some time before your tests start. I'd love to hear more about your childhood."

"There isn't very much to tell. After my grandfather gave us the new farm and we had a new house, life was pretty good. The farm gave us everything we needed. Oh, we didn't have much, but we at least had syrup for our school lunches."

"Syrup?" I asked.

"The poor kids, like your dad," she said, "they had school lunch sandwiches with lard. The kids that had more, like us, had syrup on their sandwiches.

"We had orchards and vegetables and strawberries. We spent hours and hours picking strawberries, but they sold well. We had fields of wheat. Neighbors came on thrashing day. It was a big party. Grandma cooked all day to serve lunch to everyone who came to help. There were heaps of fried chicken, corn on the cob, and lots of pie: apple pie, peach pie, or any other fruit that was ready to pick. It was the best meal of the whole year."

"Didn't you have a butchering day, like we did, when you butchered the hogs?" I asked.

"Grandpa butchered the hogs in the fall, when it was cold and we were in school," she said. "When you were young, we needed more help for butchering so we did it on weekends when our friends were off work. Grandpa sold most of the pork. We didn't eat much of it because we got lots of money for the meat; money we needed for other things. We didn't eat much beef either. We had dairy cows and sold the milk. We did get to drink some of the milk, but seldom ate beef. Beef bought things like shoes and winter coats. Important stuff." She smiled.

I think those were good memories.

"Tell me about your school," I asked.

"Oh, our school. We did actually walk two miles, even in the snow. School was never canceled for weather. Of course, there were no buses to get stuck in the snow. The only thing that stopped school was harvesting. All the kids had to work in the field during harvest. We started school early in August and then had a break in late September or October for harvest."

"Was it really all in one room?" I asked.

"One pretty small room. It was heated with an old potbelly stove. If you sat too close to the stove, you came home with one side red; if you sat at the other end of the room, you froze all day. Nobody was comfortable. We didn't have enough kids, or room, for every grade. So, on even years we had even grades: two, four, six, and eight. On odd years, we had the odd classes: one, three, five, and seven. If you fell in between years, you just jumped up to the next grade. Uncle Fred and I started the same year, even though he's a year older, because he turned six in an even year and there was no first grade. Miss Mable was our teacher. She had a big job, teaching all grades at the same time. We wrote on little slates with chalk. None of us could afford paper or pencils. We all used the same books. They were pretty worn. We read the same words over and over."

"What about homework? Did you have homework?" I asked.

"Our homework was feeding the chickens and milking the cows," she laughed. "Who had time for homework? We did schoolwork in school and farm work at home. Most of us preferred farm work. That was always easier."

"How many kids were in the school?" I asked.

"There were maybe eight families. There were three or four of us, then four or five of the Millers, three or four of the Schroeders; and the May family had a few too. Everybody knew each other.

"We walked to school with the Millers. They were really poor. Most often they wore feed-sack clothes. Lunches were pretty sad. Fred and I shared our molasses sandwiches with them. Their dad didn't know how to tend animals. Grandpa had to go help them. When we butchered, he'd take them some meat. I think that's the only meat they ever had. Everybody had patches in their clothes. We were lucky. We had an aunt who would send us coats. I don't think they were new, but who cared? We had coats. When we wore them out, Grandma sewed the pieces together to make our blankets."

"How did one teacher teach so many different classes?" I asked.

"Well, we didn't all get every lesson. Sometimes we talked about history and geography, and the little kids were mostly lost. They just listened. They would pick it up in later years."

I was so wrapped up in Mom's stories I didn't notice the attendant coming in to take Mom to her first test.

"I'll be right here when you come back," Work had sort of faded in my memory. Mom was my only concern.

Shortly after Mom left, Maria called.

"I'm tied up right now," she said. "I have a stack of bills that have to go out today. I can come in a couple of hours. How's Mom?"

"They just took her for tests," I told her casually.

"What? Didn't you go with her?" Maria said excitedly. "She gets confused. She needs to have someone there. Go find where the tests are and stay with her."

"Okay, I'm on my way," I answered grudgingly and hung up.

The last thing I wanted to do was track down Mom. Why is Maria so obsessed with over-managing Mom's care? We need to just trust the hospital. What can happen at a test anyway?

It took me four nurses to find out where Mom was. Nobody seemed to know anything. Nobody was in charge. By the time I found Mom, I was fuming. Everything was so hard. Finally, a nurse in radiology pointed to a hallway where I saw my poor, elderly mother lying on a gurney shivering. I quickly found a nurse and got a blanket.

Well, Maria was right, again. They weren't taking care of Mom while she waited for her MRI.

We sat together in the hallway for over an hour. Had I not found her, she would have been freezing all that time with no one to talk to.

Work was quickly moving further down the priority list.

"So, what did you do for fun or vacation?" I asked.

"Fun?" she asked. "Life was fun. Working on the farm, going to school, sleeping in one attic room with your siblings: that was fun. I loved picking strawberries with Uncle Fred and Aunt Martha. We always made a game of it and stole one or two to eat. They were the sweetest strawberries in the whole world. We never took a vacation. We did have sort of a field trip once when we were teenagers. We went to the amusement park, called the 'Highlands.' That was a great day. We rode every single ride. They had a great roller coaster that would scare your socks off. It was nothing like the ones today, but we thought it was wonderful.

"Oh, and one summer day, Grandpa and Grandma took us on a boat ride on the Mississippi. It was a huge boat called the 'Admiral.' Grandma packed a picnic lunch with cold chicken and her famous coffee cakes, and we all piled in the old Model T and went down to the riverfront. It was a wonderful trip. We sat on the top deck, eating our picnic lunch and watching the river towns go by. It was dark when we returned, but what a glorious day."

"That's it?" I asked, unbelieving. "That's all the vacation you ever had?"

"You sound so surprised," she smiled gently. "We never—I never had any desire to go places and see things. You only think it's strange because you want so much to travel. Maybe it's from TV. You see so many people traveling, enjoying lavish vacations as a matter of course, and think you're entitled to it. If you know you'll never have it and decide not to want it, it's no loss."

She made a lot of sense. Maybe the biggest reason many in our generation are so unhappy is because we want things we can't have and don't need. That leads to buying things, like big vacations that we can't afford, tumbling into a cavern of debt—all because we desire something we don't need. If only I could be more like her.

Finally, the testing was done. She was exhausted when we returned to her room. It's amazing how such a little thing took so much out of her drained little body. When we returned to her room, she needed to go the bathroom. Her tired legs wouldn't support her, and I didn't have the strength to lift her. We pushed the button for a nurse. Ten minutes passed, we pushed again. Another ten minutes passed. We pushed again. Mom was turning green she had to go so bad.

I walked up to the nurse's station and demanded that someone come and help Mom to the bathroom.

The head nurse came out and said, "I've got twelve patients like your mom, nonambulatory elderly, that need assistance to the toilet. I don't have enough staff to get to them all. If you think it's a problem, your mom can wear a diaper and then she can just go when she needs to."

"That's totally unacceptable," I shrieked. "You want her to learn to pee in her pants?"

"Or," said the nurse calmly, "she can wait."

Really, I thought. This is an award-winning hospital. How can they be so calloused?

I went back to find two husky orderlies man-handling my mom with a belt tied around her waist, grabbing her roughly everywhere, jerking her out of bed. Mom was crying.

"Ouch, ouch."

I quickly stepped in. "She can walk if you help her stand and give her the walker."

"We know how to do this, ma'am," he said. "We have to finish this and get the next patient."

"You can go," I snapped. Looking hard at the *kinder* orderly's badge.. "I'll help Joe with my mom.

"Okay, have it your way. Don't call me when she falls."

Joe and I managed, but it was hard. Mom was humiliated by the whole experience. All her dignity, independence, and self-reliance came crushing down in ten minutes of pulling, jerking, and pushing my mom. It was more than I could handle. I excused myself, found a bathroom, and wept.

Maria popped in the hospital door shortly. "How is everything?" she asked smiling.

"Well," Mom replied, "I was just brutalized by some hospital bullies because I had to go to the bathroom. I don't know why they had to treat me like that. I can get to the bathroom just fine. All I need is my walker."

I was trying hard to fight off tears. "You can't stand on your own, Mom. I know you could a few days ago, but you've lost a lot of balance since you've been in here. You do need some help to get to the bathroom, but they were bullies. We will have to help the orderlies so they treat you better."

I asked Maria to step into the hall. There, through tears, I told her of Mom's awful experience with the orderlies.

"I just can't handle seeing how they treat her. They have no respect for this wonderful lady. They treat her like a pile of rags."

Maria had tears streaming down her face too. "I think they treat everyone like trash," she said softly. "I have friends who work here. This hospital is understaffed. We have to be here and help. I can't bear to think how they treat her when we're gone."

"You are right, once again. Could you just be wrong once in a while?" I smiled.

Chapter 3

In the Middle

It was nearly two p.m. when I strolled into my office. I took my seat behind the pile of papers and messages and sighed heavily. I did nothing all morning but sit; but still, I felt like I had just run a marathon. I read through the notes stacked on my desk and realized I didn't remember a single thing I read. My mind was back at the hospital with Mom. I started over, trying hard to focus. About halfway through the second time, Mr. Ryan stepped into my office.

"So, you got Mommy all set up in her hospital bed," he quipped.

No way is he going to get this, so I sidestepped the issue in terms he might understand.

"She's okay. I just have to make sure that St. Mark's doesn't rip us off for anything. Those doctors don't know which way is up sometimes."

"I hear that," said Mr. Ryan. "So, did you talk to Goodman's yet?

I suspect one of the notes I hadn't read a second time yet was from my biggest account, the agency's biggest account, Goodman's Supermarket. With fifteen local grocery centers—we've long since quit calling them "grocery stores"—Goodman's was the biggest local chain in the area and the bread and butter for Ryan Advertising.

It was a big vote of confidence that Mr. Ryan let me handle this mega account. Actually, it wasn't my experience or quick wit that he used to *sell* me to Goodman's. He told them I would bring the perspective of a suburban housewife and "Mom" to the account. That's how after ten years as the agency's biggest income-earner I got the biggest account.

But now I had egg all over my face because I had no idea what he was talking about.

"I just wanted to make sure I had read all the notes before I called them," I lied.

"Well, you better get on that phone and find out what they need before we all go hungry," he smirked. "Let me know as soon as you talk with them."

Now I was reading the notes with renewed interest. Sally Brinkman, Goodman's marketing manager had left three messages.

"Sally, how can I help you?"

"Well, I guess you know what's going on," she said quickly.

Sally always started every conversation somewhere in the middle and expected I should always know everything already.

"I've been a little out of the loop this morning," I told her.

She didn't know, nor would she be interested in the details.

"Babbage's announced a big price cut this morning on meat," she said, as if the whole world knew it. "They're getting all kinds of publicity for their big effort to help working class families. We need to respond and respond fast," she added. "So, what should we do?"

"I'd like to discuss this with our creative minds. Let me give you a call back."

I actually think she really expected me to have an answer right off the top of my head. I quickly checked all the online local news sources to see what was out there. Babbage's had a pretty good idea and a good PR campaign behind it. Even though they were half the size of Goodman's, they were smart marketers, and Goodman's couldn't stand to be bested by the competition on anything.

I called a quick creative brainstorming session to gather the troops. It was obvious that Goodman's expected us to come up with a counterattack immediately.

"Okay, here's the situation."

I started nearly every meeting with this line. I had gathered our five top creatives, art director, and, of course, the omnipresent Mr. Ryan to discuss our next move for Goodman's.

After giving them the facts, I asked, "So what ideas do you have for countering Babbage's marketing move?"

I was hoping beyond hope a big idea would pop out of the sky. But I was met mostly with silence.

"Come on, gang," shouted Mr. Ryan. He always thought frightening the daylights out of his creative staff would make ideas materialize. "Give poor Carrie here something to work with. We need Goodman's."

Truth is, this marketing challenge was a potential big revenue boost to our struggling agency. Not many of the staff knew how overextended Mr. Ryan was. While he drove a Jaguar and wore Brooks Brothers, his credit card debt was extreme, both personal and for the agency. I only knew because I had to pay some of his bills when he had pneumonia last spring. But I had promised to keep silent. If we came up with an idea that would require big *off-budget* advertising spending for Goodman's, we could actually end the year in the black. The importance of a new campaign was hard to overstate.

"How about we counter by offering discounts on dairy products? Milk for children for less. What's more American and wholesome than milk?" offered George, our talented, but thick, graphic designer.

"Milk," shouted Mr. Ryan with a look that could curdle the maligned milk.

"I don't think it's a good idea to offer another discount," I pointed out. I could see everyone practically shaking by now. "It looks too much like Goodman's is simply offering a 'me-too' approach. It doesn't give them any advantage. We need something that will drive people into Goodman's, away from Babbage's, in spite of cheaper meat."

"So, what's better than cheap meat?" asked Mr. Ryan.

"A new car," said Sam Golden, art director, half joking.

"That's it. We could have a contest for a free car. We would enter your name in a drawing for a free car with every $50 purchase. Maybe give one away each month. The drawing would be a huge media event. We could have second and third prizes too," I nearly shouted.

"Would that be awfully expensive?" asked George. "I mean aren't cars like $30,000?"

"You don't actually give away the whole car. You give away a one or two year-lease. If you tie into a local dealer—give him publicity—you can get a good deal."

"I like it," said Mr. Ryan excitedly. "Let's see, we'll need new ads, a direct-mail campaign, and lots of publicity. George will prepare ad concepts. Sharon can work on direct mail, and Carrie can work up a PR campaign. I'll let Sam supervise creative, and I'll work up the client cost and contract. This is good."

"Great," said Sam. "Glad you like my idea."

Seriously? All he said was car. It was totally my idea. I was just about to say something when my cell phone rang. I looked down and saw Maria's name.

"I need to step out and take this."

"Don't take long," barked Mr. Ryan. "We've got plans to make here."

I think I actually saw steam coming from his head, but I had to see what was going on.

"Hello," I whispered into the phone, once I was in the hall.

"Carrie," said Maria, "we think Mom had a small stroke. Can you come?"

Talk about bad timing.

"Oh, Maria, that's awful, but I'm really stuck here. How bad is it? Do you think there's anything I can do?"

"Probably not, I just thought you'd want to come. Suit yourself. The doctor is pretty worried, but Mom is awake and talking. It happened while she was taking a stress test. It wasn't a big event, but pretty significant in terms of what it means for her future. I think we need to call her lawyer and get her will finalized."

Maria stopped for a minute as a little sob burst out.

"Can you at least handle that?" she said with obvious annoyance.

Can't say I blame her, I should go, but I can't. Maria won't understand this. Mom won't understand this. Mr. Ryan really won't understand if I leave. I can't win anyway at all. If I go, the whole agency will be furious; if I stay, my whole family will be mad at me. Neither will ever see the other side. I actually don't have time to talk with the lawyer, but what can I say?

"Sure, Maria, I'll call the lawyer" is what I had to say.

"I will come to the hospital as soon as I finish work," I promised. I just failed to add when I would finish.

"Okay," Maria said softly. "I'll see you then."

Maybe it would be easier if she yelled.

I quickly called the lawyer.

We had just recently discovered that Mom never had a will. I had always assumed Maria and John knew all her financial matters and was shocked to find out they were as much in the dark as I was. Money was one of those difficult issues we always managed to avoid. There was mostly enough to get by and that's all that mattered. But it had become more and more obvious in the last year that Mom was not fully in charge of all her finances. She had missed credit card payments, misplaced checks, and was not sure of any of her accounts.

I became alarmed about six months ago when she said she didn't have any money to put into the church offering. In all the years I knew her, she always had her weekly contribution carefully prepared. When the basket was passed around, she was ready. Then one week we were sitting together at church and she let the basket pass without adding her envelope. I asked if she misplaced it and she said she had no money.

After church, I called Maria and we began a search to uncover her accounts. There were funds in an annuity that we were able to transfer to her checking. But what happened to her checking account? That's when we started asking the difficult questions that we had avoided for so many years. When we discovered she had no will, we began the process of creating a living will. But it was complicated with the ownership of the farm.

The papers were finally complete, but not signed. I discovered from the lawyer, we could get the will signed, but we needed a witness and a notary. As it stood now, they'd have to both agree to go to the hospital. So, that meant more calls, coordinating schedules to get everyone to show up at the same time. By the time that was finished, it was four p.m. and I still had to create a PR campaign.

I finished a draft of the PR campaign at 6:30. Mr. Ryan had left by then, so I emailed the draft to him and left for the hospital. On the way to the hospital, Geoff called.

"Adam's game starts at seven. Shall we meet in the gym by our usual seats?"

I totally forgot Adam's basketball game. Our son is a jock. That was a total surprise. My husband and I are far from athletic. Our daughter is a total bookworm; I had to push her outside for exercise. So where did Adam come from? He made the varsity basketball team in his sophomore year. He may not be the team star, but his star was rising. Tonight is the cross-town rivalry game and I won't be there. I don't even have time to wish him well before the game. How can I ever do all this?

"I hate to say this, Geoff, but I won't make the game. I'm on the way to the hospital. Mom had a mild stroke and I need to be there."

"I understand," Geoff said. "We'll miss you. I'll tell Adam."

Geoff understands. Adam understands. But do I understand? How can I ever be there for everyone I care about?

If Mom wasn't sick, I'd be sitting at the game wolfing down some delicious popcorn and screaming with the crowd. Oh, how I do love to watch Adam play, but not tonight. Tonight, I'll sit in the hospital worrying about the rough PR campaign I threw together and what Mr. Ryan is going to scream about and how disappointed Adam will be that I missed his game and when will I ever get to spend time again with Geoff. Tonight, it's about Mom.

When I strode into Mom's room, Maria and John were there talking. Mom was sleeping.

"How is she?" I asked.

"She's doing pretty well," said Maria. "The doctor is worried, though. One more spell like this and…"

She didn't finish. Big tears were rolling down her face, John's too. Tears are contagious. Soon we were all crying.

"Let's step into the hall," I sniffed. "We don't want to wake her or let her see us like this."

When we got into the hall, emotions just poured out.

"I'm not ready to let her go," said Maria through thick tears. "I just want her with us a little longer."

"I can't let her go," said John. "I will be lost without her."

John was always the closest. He was the baby. He was *the* son. He stayed home longer than me or Maria. He was the one Mom relied on to take care of things for her. He'd fix her car or fix the plumbing or mow the grass. John is the reason Mom worked so hard to keep the farm after Dad died. He was the heir. Even though Maria and her husband ran most of it, John was Mom's favorite.

"We have to remember she has lived a good life. If it is God's plan for her to go to her heavenly home now, we will be okay," I offered

We all had very strong faith. I believed, above all else, no matter how hard this was, that heaven really was her home. It was a place with no more pain and suffering. But it doesn't diminish our grief.

"I believe that," said Maria, "but it just doesn't help much. I'm not ready."

"We are going to take care of her," said John thickly. "She can get better and we are going to see she does."

I found myself in the middle again. I was trying to look at reality, and they only wanted to hear that Mom would be fine. How can I tell them that I don't think she'll ever be the same? That's not what they want to hear.

I put an arm around each of them and pulled them together in a giant big hug. We stayed that way for minutes, tears flowing all around. Suddenly, I realized how silly this would look and I started laughing. God had given me this strange gift to see humor in the oddest places.

"You have to realize how silly this looks," I smiled. "I don't think we've group hugged since—since—"

"Since never," John laughed. "Let's not make it a habit."

With tears wiped away, we went back into Mom's room. She was waking up. Maria rubbed her arm gently.

"How are you feeling, Mom?" she asked.

"Oh, I'm okay," she said. "But this bed is not as comfortable as my bed at home. When can I go home?"

"It's going to be a couple more days," Maria answered.

"We don't want you to come home until you're completely healed," John added.

"I don't think I need the hospital," Mom said. "I think I'd get better faster in my own house, in my own bed. I need to go to the bathroom. Help me up."

"We really should get an attendant," Maria said. "I'll push the button for the nurse."

We were having a nice discussion about childhood times, when I realized it had been fifteen minutes and no reply to our buzzing. I stepped out in the hall and asked a nurse for assistance.

"What do you need?" she asked.

"My mother needs help getting to the bathroom," I said as politely as possible.

"You'll have to wait until two orderlies are available," she snapped.

"And exactly how does an eighty-two-year-old lady wait to go to the bathroom?" I asked a little too sharply.

"The best she can, I suppose," the nurse replied walking away.

"I think we need to take Mom to the bathroom ourselves," I snarled as I walked back in the room.

"That's fine," said John. "We can do this."

And together we did, slowly, tenderly, but with great difficulty.

Mom quickly fell asleep when she had finished and the three of us moved our discussion to the lounge.

"If it's going to be that hard to get Mom to the bathroom," John said, "how can she live alone?"

"I don't think she can," I replied. "I think we need to look into options."

"Do you know how much *options* cost?" asked Maria. "I'm not ready for Mom to be in a nursing home. I think we can take care of her."

"What if we took turns staying with her?" said John. "At least we could try. I have no money to spend on a nursing home. We have to work together and give this a try."

I wanted to say, *But I have a job, I have kids, I have a life.* I really didn't have that much of a life, but I wasn't quite willing to give up what I did have.

"I know this is what Mom says she wants; but do you think, five or ten years ago when her mind was better, she would have chosen this for us?" I asked.

I can't imagine the mother who gave everything for us would want us to give up so much for her. Or was that just my selfishness showing through?

"It doesn't matter," said Maria. "We *have* to do this. It's not a choice. There is no money for a decent nursing home, and what there is, we may need later on, if…things get worse."

There was silence for a few minutes. Then Maria spoke again.

"The first thing we need to do is clean up her house and make some changes for her return. Have either of you been in there lately? It's pretty awful. She'll need plenty of room to wheel the walker to get around, and we'll have to make changes to her bedroom and bathroom."

"And," added John, "if we're staying there, we need to clean out the back bedroom. She's managed to pile everything that came in the door in the last ten years in that room. It will take some effort to make it livable."

As I was driving home that evening, I suddenly felt a strange ache in my stomach. With all the emotional turmoil of the day, I had completely forgotten my stomach. That ache was hunger. Food. Meals had become so unimportant. The one true staple in my life was so easily forgotten. At that moment, I knew life as I knew it would never be the same again. I had a new focus, taking care of Mom, and everything else was second. What we had discussed that evening was the beginning of whole new order of life.

The plan was set. Our journey just beginning.

Chapter 4
Moving On

It was nearly noon when I strode into the office the next day. I had completed my shift with Mom including two battles to get her to the bathroom with the orderlies. But I made a new friend. Joe, the kind orderly, who, the day before, had agreed to help me take Mom to the toilet ourselves. He was the one person on Mom's floor that I could count on to listen to us.

I called Maria and told her to look for Joe during her watch. I was trying to remember what else I should have told Maria as I sat at my desk.

"Glad you could make it," barked Mr. Ryan. "Have you checked your messages?"

Of course, I hadn't. To be honest, my head was still in the hospital.

"I'm getting on that now,"

"Well, when you get around to it," said Mr. Ryan, sarcastically, "you'll find an irate call from Sally Brinkman about your lack of response to her big Babbage problem and one from me on the half-assed PR campaign you left me. Evidently, I didn't sufficiently impress on you the importance of this opportunity. I expect you here at your desk until the client and I are thrilled with our response."

"Yes, sir. Got it," I replied. My anger was building so rapidly, I thought it might explode out the top of my head. I had a good idea. No, a great idea. I left a good plan on his desk. What more did he want? Blood?

"Can you tell me what was wrong with my plan?" I asked.

"First, get Sally on the phone, *now!*" He bellowed so the whole cubical jungle heard. That was no accident. He clearly wanted everyone to know how angry he was.

I quickly picked up the phone and dialed Sally. Sally and I first met when our agency bid for Goodman's account. I always thought our immediate chemistry had something to do with winning the account. Of course, Mr. Ryan thought it was all his doing. He was convinced Mrs. Goodman was *hot* for him. Please! She's a smart lady with more than a little taste.

Sally's voice mail picked up. Oh, how I hate answering machines. They're the nemeses of my business. I'm not letting voice mail keep me from finding Sally and fixing this problem.

I called her assistant and explained the urgency of my need to talk to Sally. After some coaxing, she gave me a number where I could reach her. She was spending the afternoon with her son and had her personal cell with her. I didn't know she had a personal cell.

We had grown quite close. Our lunches were always a great time. We had so much in common. We both had kids past the tweens. She was a single mom, but I enjoyed listening to her dating adventures. It was like living this exciting, adventurous life through Sally. Truthfully, I'd never do some of the things she did even if I was single, but I couldn't help fanaticizing about the *other side.*

Nobody at Ryan Advertising understood where I was coming from. I was well aware that behind my back they called me "the church lady." Ironically, I got a certain amount of pleasure from their nickname.

"Hello, this is Sally."

Finally, I connected.

"What can I do for you?"

"Hi, Sally, this is Carrie. I'm sorry I didn't get back to you this morning. My mom's in the hospital. I want to talk to you about our plan to counter Babbage's campaign."

"Carrie," she said rather sharply. "I've taken the afternoon off to spend some time with my son. I'm surprised you got this number. I am anxious to see your plan. I was in the office all morning waiting for your call. I'll be there tomorrow morning starting at seven. If you have something to show me, why don't you come to my office, say, eight a.m.?"

"Great. I'll see you at eight and I'll bring the bagels."

A little schmoozing can't hurt.

"That won't be necessary," she said a little too coldly. "We have a lot to do. See you at eight."

The phone was dead, but I couldn't quite bring myself to hang up. Sally is my friend, isn't she? Why is she mad at me? I wanted to call back and say, *Did I tell you my mom was in the hospital?* But I know I did. She either didn't hear or didn't care. I had to talk this out with someone.

I chose Jamie the office manager and my assistant. We were sort of friends. She was much younger than me and single but nice, or so I thought. She always had her ear to office gossip and knew everything. I was just the opposite, completely clueless on office rumors. Maybe that's because I really didn't care. I had plenty to care about with two growing kids and my full extended family. I simply chose to politely ignore them.

I was still in a bit of a daze when I strolled up to Jamie's desk.

"I just had the oddest conversation with Sally Brinkman. She was pretty mad. I just can't figure it out."

"Really," mused Jamie. "You didn't know she was steaming over you being out all morning for the last two days?"

"But you told her my mom was in the hospital, didn't you?"

Now I was really starting to feel sick.

"You never gave me the authority to give out personal information to clients. I'm sorry if I overstepped," said Jamie, rather coolly. "I just told her you were out for the morning on personal business. When she insisted on talking to someone, I handed her over to Mr. Ryan. He was pleased that I took charge of the matter," she added.

"And yesterday when I was at the hospital, did you tell her the same thing?" I asked.

"Of course," she replied, smiling.

My mind was racing. Jamie did what she thought was right, didn't she? Sally was angry because Jamie left out a key piece of information about why I was absent. From her perspective, I had been totally unresponsive to a crisis. I couldn't make an excuse with Sally now. It was way too late.

I strode back to my desk with my heart in my throat. What now? Is Jamie on my side or not? I just wasn't sure. Between trying to deal with Mom issues, the Goodman's crisis, and missing Adam's great game last night, I was in no mood to play office politics. Truth is, I've never been a game-player. Everybody knew that's why I had never risen higher in the advertising world. I was okay just doing my job. Maybe that wasn't enough. But right now, I was feeling more like an all-around failure. I think I just have to give Jamie the benefit of the doubt. Then my cell rang. It was Maria.

"Listen, they're going to do more tests tomorrow morning. I'm really concerned about it. They want to give Mom a stress test, but she can't walk. The doctor says they can do a chemical stress test, but I don't think this is going to work. Can you be here tomorrow morning?" she asked.

"I'm so sorry, Maria, but I can't." I knew this was not what Maria wanted to hear. It's not what I wanted to say either. But there it was. "I have a meeting in the morning I can't get out of. Can you cover?"

"I promised Katie I'd go to the ob-gyn with her tomorrow. She's getting an ultrasound and may know the sex of her baby." Maria said.

Maria's daughter, Katie, was three months pregnant with baby number three. She had some blood clot issues with baby number two so this was a little scary. Katie had two lovely girls but dearly wanted a boy. I know Maria needed to be there for her daughter, but what could I do?

"How about John?" I asked.

"John has to take a load of pumpkins to Springfield tomorrow. You know this is our peak season. What doesn't sell in the next few weeks we can throw out." she pleaded.

"I'll try to get my meeting moved to ten o'clock."

"Okay, but this is important, you know," she said curtly.

"I know," I said softly.

After I hung up, I took a couple of deep breaths. This was going to be hard. I had to call Sally and see if she could move our meeting to ten. No point in waiting. Like ripping off the bandage, I had to just pick up the phone and make the call. I got Sally's assistant. She said ten would be fine. Actually, she thought ten might be better. Good, I was halfway there.

Now I have to put together a dazzling proposal. I feel like I am failing at everything: my career, as a mother, as a daughter, as a person.

Just start, I thought, one word at a time.

I was making good progress. I checked with the creative team, and they had some great graphics to go with the proposal. Maybe this was going to work. Maybe I wasn't a total failure. This was going to take some time. I knew I couldn't leave until the whole thing was done. My proposal was shaping up. Just one question left, who could I rely on to be on my side?

It was nine p.m. The creative team had completed their work an hour ago and left. I just went through everything one more time to make sure it was perfect. Then packed it up and headed for home.

That strange ache deep in my stomach was raising its ugly head again. Eating had become so unimportant, except my stomach hadn't forgotten food. Just one more neglected part of my life.

As I pulled into a McDonald's for a quick burger, I thought about all the great meals I had made for my family. I loved to cook and always prided myself on providing nutritious, delicious meals. When would I make a family meal again? Geoff had been so good about this. He brought home a pizza for him and Adam tonight. How many more pizzas would they have to eat?

The alarm was way too early again. Sleep had not come quickly. My head was swirling with so many thoughts—the presentation, the tests, Jamie. But it had been a long day, and sleep came. And now it was time to face another morning.

I was up and out the door before Adam awoke. Geoff had promised to stay and see he got off to school. St. Mark's Hospital was starting to feel familiar now. I managed to grab a muffin and coffee on the way in. I got to Mom's room at seven; she was sitting up enjoying a carefully selected breakfast of indistinguishable flavorless food.

"I came to have breakfast with you," I said cheerfully.

"I'd rather have what you're having," Mom said, smiling. "You didn't have to get up so early to babysit me. I'll be fine. I think I'm going home today anyway." Then added, "Don't you have a job?"

Oh, boy, do I have a job? Do I want to be here? Does she even want me here?

"I came to see you before work because I love you."

It was mostly true. I wouldn't get up at the crack of dawn if she wasn't ill. As a matter of fact, when she was doing well on her own, I hardly ever visited outside of major holidays. So, she was right to wonder at my sudden interest in sharing breakfast. Time to change the subject.

"Did you sleep well last night?" I asked.

"No not very well," she answered. "There's too much light, too many nurses poking on you, and way too many lumps this bed. And the sheets are so slick, they keep sliding off the bed. I need to get home. There's pumpkins to harvest and apples to pick. They need me on the farm."

Mom hadn't done any of these things in years, but still she thought none of it would happen without her. It's understandable. After Dad died, Mom had taken care of all these things for years. It had become her life. She rarely did anything else. Letting go was hard. Time for another subject.

"I bet sleeping in your comfortable bed when you were a kid was more fun," I mused, thinking I'd bring up a more pleasant subject.

"Ha," she said. "Hardly. We were all squeezed into a little loft with a straw mattress spread on the floor. Whoever was the baby slept in the room with Grandma and Grandpa. By the time there were four of us, it got pretty crowded. But it helped us stay warm in the winter. That old house was so poorly built; the wind blew right in between the boards. On snowy mornings, you could wake with snow next to you. Our blankets were made from old coats sewn together. I guess they kept us warm because we never froze. In summer though, oh, in summer it would be so hot. Sometimes we slept on the porch, but the bugs could practically carry you away."

"Couldn't you use a fan?" I asked squirming at the thought of the heat in that attic room.

"Fan, ha! Fan," she laughed. "We didn't even have electricity, much less a fan. We could have made a paper fan, but someone had to make it work. The best thing to do when you woke up cold was get yourself downstairs and eat breakfast. The old potbelly stove in the kitchen put out a might lot of heat. But if you sat too close, you might burn your buns. Not the breakfast kind."

She was laughing again. How good to hear her laugh.

I looked down at my watch and it was 8:30. We were having such a good time, I completely forgot about the time. I excused myself and went out to the nurse's station to check on the test. It took about ten minutes to find a nurse and another ten for her to look up Mom's chart.

"It looks like the doctor must be delayed," she said. "I assume an orderly will be in for her shortly."

"But," I pleaded, "I have to leave at 9:30. The test was supposed to be done by then. I need to be here for the test."

"I can't tell you when it will happen or when it will be done. There is really no need for you to be here. Stay if you want."

That's it. That's all I get. Just stay. There isn't enough time left this morning to explain to this nurse how hard that is. *Just stay.* Can anything ever be that easy? So much emotion busting up I couldn't hold it in. I couldn't get any words out any more than I could stop the tears.

The nurse looked at me more out of disgust than anything else. "Sorry" was all she could offer. She turned and walked away.

I had no choices left. No options. Maria wasn't going to be happy about this. Maybe I could just avoid telling her altogether. Right now, she was on her way to the doctor's office with Katie and her two little girls. I was not calling her now. John was halfway to Springfield. Not calling him either. Maybe the nurse was right about not needing to be here. Maybe I could just talk to the doctor after. I quickly ran after the nurse.

She turned sharply, expecting maybe a confrontation.

"If I leave before the test," I asked, "how I can find out what happened?"

"You'll have to call the doctor," she told me. "I'll get his card for you." I think she was relieved I wasn't asking more.

I walked back into the room to find a nursing student abusing my mom with a needle. Mom's face was all contorted as he dug deep into her arm, presumably looking for a vein.

"What are you doing?" I demanded.

"I need to take some blood before her stress test," he answered, a little red from being caught bumbling a blood draw.

"Oh no, you don't," I said as firmly as I could manage. "My mother is not a pin cushion. If you can't do this, you'll have to get someone else."

I was actually surprised at how authoritative I sounded.

"Yes, ma'am," he said and tottered off.

Mom's face was still grimaced.

"I'm so sorry about that. I can't believe they sent a student in here when your veins are so hard to find."

"Thank you," she said finally. "I didn't know you could make him find someone else. It hurt so much."

I came over to her side of the bed and hugged her.

The IV tech came into the room and said, smiling, "So I hear you're a hard stick. I'll have this done in no time." And she did. It's amazing the difference between an amateur and a professional.

"I'm so grateful. I don't want a student torturing my mom."

"I understand," she replied. "I'll put on her chart that she needs an IV tech. Next time, they should call me first. If someone else comes ask for me."

I looked down at my watch. It was 9:30. I had to fly. I kissed Mom goodbye and raced down the hall. Before I took off, I checked messages. Nothing. I was okay. I didn't check my office messages because I was sure that Jamie would call my cell if there were any changes. I strode into Sally's office to a very surprised look on her assistant's face.

"Didn't you get my message?" she asked looking very puzzled. "I talked to your receptionist this morning and told her Sally was not okay with moving the meeting to ten o'clock. She would like you to come at one o'clock. Is that okay?"

"Of course, I'll see you at one." I quickly exited turning a dark shade of purple.

What was Jamie thinking? Should I ignore this? I had to confront Jamie. I couldn't process this. I thought we were friends, or at least friendly. She liked the little globe I brought her from my Florida trip.

If I told Mr. Ryan, wouldn't it look like I couldn't handle my account? No matter how I played the conversation over in my head, saying, *Mr. Ryan, Jamie's not giving me my messages,* it would sound like I was ten. I played the messages on my work line. There it was.

I couldn't tell Mr. Ryan that Jamie had left the message where she knew I wouldn't look. Doesn't he always say, "Be sure to check office messages." Only Jamie knew I never checked the office messages before I got to the office. She knew I wouldn't know the meeting was changed unless she called my cell phone. But I could never prove it. She knew that too.

Once more, I had to rip off a Band-Aid. Mr. Ryan would be furious that I didn't meet with Goodman's today. It was my turn for more abuse; and once again, I was powerless against Jamie's move. As I walked into the office, Mr. Ryan was waiting.

"So how did the meeting go?" he asked anxiously.

"It didn't," adding quickly before he reached the boiling stage. "It's been postponed to one o'clock today. I thought Jamie would tell you."

"Well, Jamie's not the hotshot account exec, is she?" He asked sarcastically. "It's your job to tell me it was postponed."

My little jab at Jamie didn't work. Why did I think it would? This is not my game.

I dropped my stuff on my desk. I needed to call Maria and let her know what happened with Mom.

"It's a boy," Maria nearly screamed into the phone. "We're so excited. Everything looks great too. Katie is elated. How did Mom's test go?"

Rip, another Band-Aid.

"They postponed the test and I had to leave. I've got the doctor's card though. We can call and talk to him."

"Oh, Carrie, I was counting on you," she sighed. "Give me the doctor's number. I'll call him."

I could handle this, but I'd never convince her now. I felt like I was six again and my big sister was scolding me for some childhood infringement. I read the number off the card. She's better at this stuff than me anyway, I thought.

One o'clock came and the presentation went off without a hitch. There were no fireworks afterwards, though. Somewhere in my imagination, I had a vision of Sally jumping from her chair throwing confetti and announcing that this was the best presentation of an idea in modern history. But that didn't happen. Sally acknowledged that it was a good idea, but she would have to "take it under advisement." That was neither good nor bad. But I wanted an answer and got none. I had absolutely nothing to tell Mr. Ryan.

It was nearly three o'clock when I returned to the office. Mr. Ryan was out at a meeting with his big client. I quietly sat at my desk pondering the events of this week and wondering when I would get my life back.

My cell phone rang. The caller ID displayed "Maria." I stared at it for just a moment. What would happen if I simply didn't answer? That phone started all this trouble, didn't it? Could I turn back the clock and erase all the problems of this week if I just ignored the phone?

"Hello." Was it really me that answered the enemy?

"Well, I spoke to the doctor," Maria drove me right back into the abyss. Maybe it was Maria's fault. "Mom passed the stress test, if you can call it passing. Her heart is good, just surrounded by fluid. In a couple more days, she will be well enough to come home, but she's greatly weakened. She'll need a walker or maybe even wheelchair to get around, and her diet will have to change dramatically. No more sodium. That will be hard. We'll have to watch her carefully the first week or two. I think if you and John meet me at the house about seven Saturday morning and we work through the weekend, we should be able to clean her house enough for her to navigate with a walker and make a place for one of us to stay."

I was listening to Maria. I know she was saying words or making noise, but I just didn't want to hear her. Things were bad enough. Could she just leave me alone? The juggernaut was rolling and I couldn't even slow it down.

"I have you staying Tuesday night. If you get up and give her breakfast, you can be in your office by nine or ten at the latest. John and I will take the rest of the week and you can take the next weekend. How will that work?"

Terrible! I wanted to shout. *Don't you see I'm trying to get my life back, not take more away. I don't want to be in this storm. I want out. How can I lose two weekends right in the middle of basketball season, right in the heart of battle with my biggest client? NO, NO, NO!*

"Sure, that sounds fine" is what I said. "I really need to work tomorrow. I'll see Mom tomorrow night and then meet you Saturday morning."

Was that really me agreeing to this insanity? I heard myself speaking, but I'm not sure what I actually said.

Mr. Ryan broke my haze.

"I just talked to Sally at Goodman's. She said she liked your proposal and so did Mrs. Goodman. We did it. I expect you in early tomorrow. We have lots of work to do."

Suddenly, my brain caught up to my ears and Mr. Ryan's words were registering, but something wasn't right.

"I'm surprised Sally didn't call me.".

"Oh, she did, but Jamie said you were on a personal call and put her through to me. That Jamie, always thinking, heh?"

Yes, Jamie. Always thinking.

Chapter 5

Moving Home

I was in the office at seven the next morning. We made great strides on the new marketing campaign for Goodman's by the time I limped out at 6:30 p.m. After a short visit with Mom, I managed to catch the last half of Adam's game. He looked great. I missed his first ten points, but managed to see his last eight. I was hoping he didn't notice I was late. Life felt a little more normal. At least until I rolled out of bed the next morning at six.

Geoff couldn't believe any sane person would give up a perfectly good Saturday to clean their mother's house, especially when their own house needed it just as much. But he was a good trooper and agreed to do some of our weekly Saturday chores alone. I treated myself to a vanilla latte on the way to Mom's in hopes of improving my mood. I was going, but I wasn't going to like it.

It had been months since I was at Mom's house. She had long since given up the big parties at her house. She couldn't cook anymore like in her younger days. Back then the smells from her kitchen would find me twenty miles away. The memory of her apple pie made my mouth water. But, lately, she mostly made messes. Even her famous banana cake sank. She couldn't get through a recipe without forgetting an important ingredient. Everything tasted like something essential was missing. She spilled eggs, cartons of milk, bowls of flour—pretty much everything she picked up. But she hadn't attempted anything for months, or so I thought.

I met Maria and John just as they were walking in the front door. A foul smell nearly knocked us over when we opened the door. Nothing could have prepared us for what we saw. Rotten or rotting food was everywhere: on the counter, on the table, on the floor, in the sink. Broken eggs, spilled soup, buckets of God-only-knows-what. Spoiled milk sat in cups and gallon jugs. Dishes caked with oatmeal and potato and stuff we wouldn't dare guess at.

We walked through the mess to the living room. It was not much better here. There were piles and piles of newspapers, magazines, and junk mail. Here and there were packages of useless stuff she had ordered from catalogs. Clean wash, dirty wash, pieces of past clothing—so worn it was mostly holes—was spread everywhere. Cobwebs hung thick in every corner.

Maria pushed aside some dirty laundry to sit on the sofa and put her head in her hands. John sat on the first thing that would hold him. I was frozen to the spot.

"Hasn't anyone been in to see her lately?" I asked. "How long has it been since someone was here?"

Maria's house was just a country block away. Years ago, when Maria and her husband took over the farm, they built next door, country style. I always assumed she checked in on Mom regularly. Maybe not.

John spoke first, "You know, it's apple and pumpkin time. It's our busy season. We work around the clock. This time of year, we can't check on Mom every day. Most of the time, she's in the store helping out. Not this year, though. She wasn't feeling well and just stayed in the house. I guess the weeks went by before we knew anything was wrong."

"I knew she wasn't well," Maria sighed. "I thought she just had a cold or flu. She never said it was worse. She never asked for any help. Even when we went to the hospital, she walked over to my house to tell me. I haven't been in here in weeks."

"It's not our fault. We didn't know how sick she was. There's no point in beating ourselves up. We couldn't help if she didn't ask for it.

All we can do is make sure we watch her more carefully in the future. We will never be able leave her on her own again.". Even though I said it, I wasn't sure the gravity and the consequences of this statement had fully sunk in. "There's not much time to think about it. We've got to get to work. We only have two days before she comes home."

"How about we start with a prayer?" Maria suggested.

It was a great idea. We prayed for Mom and for the strength to complete our task.

"You know," said Maria, "she's not going to like that we've messed with her stuff."

"We'll just have to deal with that when she comes home," John said as he picked up a pile of magazines. "I'll carry some of this stuff to my truck and haul it to the recycling center."

We followed John's lead and each carried an arm full of papers out to his truck. Then, bit by bit we tackled the mess. At five p.m. we decided we had had enough for the day and returned to our families to salvage a little weekend.

We started again on Sunday after church. Maria and I teach Sunday School together at the church we had attended as children. So, we came to Mom's house a little tired, but had to finish. We cleaned up all the messes in the kitchen and dining room, washed all the dishes and dirty laundry, found a home for everything on the counters, floors and tables, and vacuumed and washed floors. We moved furniture to make sure Mom could negotiate with her new walker. We made sure a wheelchair could navigate through the rooms, just in case. We also made a clean space for one of us to stay. We uncovered the bed in the room Maria and I shared as kids.

Standing in this room brought back so many memories, like the day we moved into this beautiful house. This house seemed like a castle to my ten-year-old self. Maria and I had been sharing a pull-out sofa in the living room of our three-room shack. It had no bathroom and no running water. This house was like a dream. Maria and I shared a whole room to ourselves and we each had our own bed. And we had not one but two bathrooms. What joy that was.

Since we left home, Mom had used our room as a general dumping ground for years. It was piled with forgotten Christmas presents, old clothes, and abandoned toys. Once the piles were stored and the linens washed, it was more livable. By eight p.m. we were totally exhausted. But one more task remained. We had to set a calendar for who would stay with Mom when.

This was going to put a deep hole in my work schedule. Maria and John were kind. They agreed to cover the first week. I would take care of Mom on Friday, plus the weekend. I argued that we needed some professional help to do things like bathe her. Maria insisted no stranger would bathe our mom. She volunteered to do it. Neither John nor I were willing to take that step. I really didn't think Maria should either. She wasn't young. She had back trouble and hip trouble. But she was determined. One thing I've learned over the years, when Maria is determined, just step back.

It all looked good on paper, but didn't leave me much time for my family. I drove home and collapsed into bed.

I was flying though Mom's house in a floating, transparent night dress. The room was filled with fog as I flew down and picked up some trash and flew away. I struggled to pick up one piece of trash that was glued to floor. Dad told me I had to pick it up quick because Mom was coming.

"Get up, Carrie," I heard Geoff yell through the fog. "Your alarm went off ages ago."

I opened my eyes and bolted from the bed. "Why did you let me sleep so late?" I screamed.

"Why did I let you?" he repeated. "I've been trying to get you up for the last half hour. You were dead to the world."

"No. I was flying." Geoff just stared at me.

Not only was I thirty minutes late to work the next morning, but I managed to top that by asking for Friday off.

"Going fishing?" Mr. Ryan asked. "Or just tired of the old salt mine?"

"I have to take care of my mom. Does it matter? You know I wouldn't ask if it wasn't important."

"Well," he smirked, "I guess everybody has a different way of deciding what's important. See, my dear old momma is in a nursing home with real nurses taking care of her so I can do my work."

"Yes," I shot back. "I suppose everybody does have a different way of deciding what and who is important."

I wondered how long we would be able to keep up this tug-of-war before he gets tired of it all and lets me go.

Back at my desk I had plenty to think about, the least of which was my work. Should we just put Mom in a nursing home? How much were we expected to give up in order to take care of her? Weren't the people in the nursing homes trained for that? What did I know about caring for an obstinate, uncooperative elderly patient? But on the other hand, what had she given up for me? All those years she ran the farm by herself after Dad died. She had options, but she stayed and kept the farm running. She didn't have to help me through college. Lord knows she had better things to do with her money. And while she may be obstinate and uncooperative and at times outside reality, she was my mother. In a nursing home, she'd be just another number, another crabby old lady. I knew her at her best and worst and loved her for all the things she was, even half crazy.

No, Mr. Ryan, you are wrong. The nursing home is not for my mother, at least, not yet. We had to try.

I knew this would reduce what little value I had to the agency, but this was not the only job in the city. Neither Mr. Ryan nor this job would keep me from doing what I knew was right. After all, wasn't this one of God's commandments? "Honor they father and mother." God didn't say, "Only as long as they are healthy or as long as it fits into your work schedule." I knew what I had to do.

Work went extremely well all week. With my decision firmly made, even sleeping was easier.

Maria said Mom was far from happy about our cleaning project. She had complained all day about how we threw out important things. She couldn't find anything anymore. While that was true, it wasn't from our cleaning. It was more likely her memory, which is the thing she really had lost.

Friday came far too soon. It was my turn to stay with Mom, but I wasn't quite ready. I wanted Mom to have some great meals while I was staying with her, but finding the ingredients for salt-free meals was harder and more expensive than I could have imagined. I had to go to a high-priced health-food store and stayed up until eleven p.m. cooking. It took nearly an hour to pack up all the things I bought, made, and planned to make with pans and spices. I packed my clothes for two days on the farm, plus church on Sunday. I have gone on week-long vacations with less preparation. But, at last, I was on my way.

My cell phone was ringing. It was John.

"Where are you Carrie? You were supposed to be here so I could go to work. I need to leave."

"I'm so sorry, John. I'll be there in thirty minutes or less. Just put Mom in her living room chair and I'll give her breakfast when I get there. It will be all right," I promised.

When I got to Mom's, John had already left. Mom was sitting in her living room chair just staring at the wall. I rushed in thinking of the worst, but she was just sitting.

"Hi, Mom. Why don't you turn on the TV?"

"I don't like TV," she said, "except for the evening news and that show about the family that's so funny."

"Well, why don't I find something for you to watch?" I asked.

I love watching TV. I would like nothing more than watching TV all day. Surely, I could teach my mom to like watching TV too.

"Turn that thing off!" she demanded. "It's a waste of time. There is so much to do. You do know this is apple-picking time? We have to get out there and sell some apples and pumpkins. Maria and John can't do it all themselves," she said.

Oh, boy, I wasn't prepared for this. She must know that she couldn't stand for hours in the apple store selling produce. She can't even stand up on her own.

"Mom, why don't I fix you breakfast?" I asked.

"Didn't John fix breakfast?" she asked.

"No, Mom. John had to leave for work, but I'm here. Can I make you some eggs?"

"I always eat oatmeal," Mom replied. "Maria knows I eat oatmeal. Maria can make me oatmeal."

"Maria's not here today either, but I can make oatmeal."

"You don't know how to make oatmeal," she said again. "Call Maria. She'll tell you how."

There was a voice ringing in my ear that said, *Call Maria and have her tell you how to make oatmeal. Just humor Mom.* But I wanted to handle this on my own. I couldn't call Maria every time I didn't know what to do. I had to figure things out. I can do this.

"Mom, how could I be married twenty-five years, raise two kids, and not know how to make oatmeal?" I asked.

"You're married twenty-five years? Well, you don't know how I make it."

"Okay, Mom. Why don't you tell me how to make oatmeal?" This *is* her house. Let her be the boss.

"Get the big round box from the pantry. Don't use water like the box says. I always use milk. It's creamier that way. And don't cook it in the microwave. It tastes much better if you cook it on the stove, just like I did when you were little. That's the way I always make it."

"Okay, Mom. I'm making it your way." I took out a pan and started measuring. I over cooked the oatmeal a little, like I always do on the stove, but it was pretty good. Mom ate it all. One little victory.

After breakfast Mom said, "I think I had an accident last night in my bedroom. Maybe you should call Maria. She'll know how to clean it up."

I walked into the bedroom. The smell of urine hit me as soon as I opened the door. Nice of John to leave this bit out, I thought. The bed was wet, the floor was wet, and her night clothes were wet, as were yesterday's clothes lying on the floor. We had put a port-a-potty next to Mom's bed because she couldn't walk to the toilet in the night. It appeared that she tried to make it to the port-a-potty but missed by a mile.

I stripped the bed and got a bucket and mop. As I started cleaning, Mom came by with her walker.

"You have to use bleach on the floor," she said. "And when you wash the sheets, make sure you add Borateem, nothing else, just Borateem," she said.

I did as she asked, but when I got to the laundry room, there was no Borateem. I don't think she's used Borateem since we were kids. I started the washing machine and then stopped it. Mom was so insistent on this, if I use the wrong stuff, she'll know. Time to call Maria.

It worked. Maria knew what Mom used and where it was. One save for Maria.

When I came upstairs from the laundry room, Mom was trying to put on her coat and hat.

"Mom, where are you going?" I asked.

"I'm going to the apple store," she replied. "Did you see how many cars are in the parking lot? They're going to need my help."

From Mom's house, you could see the apple store parking lot and it was indeed packed. The last thing they needed now was Mom.

"It's time for lunch now. We don't want to bother them during lunch. Let's eat first, then we'll go."

"Okay," Mom allowed. "Can we have some tomato soup for lunch? John wouldn't make tomato soup, but that's what I always eat."

"We've had this discussion, Mom. You can only eat things low in salt, and that doesn't include tomato soup. But I made some vegetable soup at home last night. Why don't you try that?"

"Do you have okra in your vegetable soup? I always use okra. I like lima beans and cabbage. Do you have cabbage?"

I can do this. I can do this, I kept repeating to myself.

"Mom, is there okra and lima beans in your freezer?" I asked.

Mom froze vegetables from her garden every year, but rarely used them anymore.

"Yes, I think there is. And there should be cabbage in the garden."

I found the okra, lima beans—a couple of years old, but still okay—and cabbage and added them to the soup. Another success.

After a delicious, if salt-free, lunch, I sat Mom in the living room chair again. I was hoping she had forgotten the promise to go to the apple store, so I thought I would quickly get her mind on something else.

"When you were in the hospital, you were talking about your childhood. What did you do when you finished school?" I asked.

"When I graduated from eighth grade, there weren't many options for us farm girls." She began. "The only high school was in the city. That was miles away and we didn't have any way to get there. I wanted to go, but it was expensive and far away.

"My cousins, Laura and Emma, were maids. They made good money, almost five dollars a week, and got to live in these big houses. So, I got a job as a maid too. I walked four miles every Sunday to the trolley and rode it to Kirkwood. There, I walked two miles to the Augustines' house. Mr. Augustine owned a factory that made barrels for beer and shipping. It was a booming business.

"The house was so grand. There were three floors and six bedrooms. The third floor had two small children's playrooms and a grand ballroom. They hardly ever used that; and the Augustine children would play up there, roller skating and running around in the big room. I spent hours and hours cleaning silver, scrubbing floors, and cooking."

"You were a cook?" I asked, astonished.

"Why so surprised? There weren't many trained chefs in those days. I learned from Mrs. Augustine and her cook. She always said it's better to get someone young and teach her your methods.

"I learned so many things your grandma couldn't teach me. That's how I learned to make the oil pie crust and yeast coffee cakes. I would get up at four every morning to have fresh bread and coffee cakes for their breakfast. They wouldn't be caught dead eating oatmeal. That was poor-man's food, as was almost everything I knew of.

"Mrs. Augustine did everything with great flair. They had wonderful dinner parties. I worked my fingers to the bone, but it was fun living in this big house with so many lovely things; things we knew nothing of back on the farm. I learned to rub the wood bowls with garlic and oil for salad. I didn't even know what salad was before I worked there. On the farm we only ate what was in season, but the Augustines had summer vegetables in the middle of winter and citrus in summer. They served pheasant or lamb with mounds of roasted potatoes. And they had fruit I had never even heard of. They made ice cream in the middle of the week. We made deviled eggs from little quail eggs. The tables were covered in fine Irish linen that we spent hours ironing with an iron heated on the wood stove. It was so elegant. We even served little bowls of water to wash their fingers.

"Every week we had to carefully clean the silver and crystal and return each item to its spot in the huge pantry. Saturday mornings, I rode back to the farm on the trolley for one night, then back to the city on Sunday evenings."

Before long, she fell asleep sitting in her big chair. I took the opportunity to take a stroll around the farm. It had changed quite a bit since I was young, but there were still so many memories here.

My parents had saved every penny during the first ten years of their marriage and bought this farm with cash. Dad built a building that was supposed to be a work shed and ran out of money, so we lived in that shed for ten years. I was born the first year they lived here.

Dad loved farming. He planted stuff he knew about: fruit trees, melons, pumpkins, and vegetables. The orchards grew and grew. He had greenhouses for vegetable plants and seedlings. He mostly sold the produce to the wholesale markets, but we always sold a few to locals. Of course, we had cows, pigs, and chickens too, mostly for our own use. Occasionally, we sold eggs or sausage.

Dad died when I was sixteen, and Mom struggled hard to keep the farm running. We had pretty hard times. Maria always wanted to work on the farm and got a degree in agriculture. That's where she met her husband, Bill. They were only married a couple of years when Mom asked them to come and take over. John was still a teenager. Mom knew it would be a long time before he was ready for a leading role on the farm, and she needed help. Mom worked her fingers to the bone, but she was never good at business.

Bill made a lot of changes. He started the apple store and developed a brand around the Schmidt Farms' name. He had great fall festivals that drew large crowds of city people to the farm to pick apples and pumpkins. In the summer, he had peach-picking picnics. It worked well, but the business was heavily centered on the crop seasons. If the weather was not on our side, the season could be dismal.

The business needed a lot of labor and reaped little profit. So, it was a yearly battle with the bankers to keep the place running. Mom, of course, knew little about this. She saw crowds in the store and thought they were making lots of money. Truth was they were barely scraping by.

I got back to the house just as Mom was waking up. I told her I had planned a special dinner. I had bought lovely T-bone steaks that I broiled. I had Martha Steward recipes for salad, broccoli au gratin, and duchess potatoes. For dessert, I made little pots of cream of cocoa with Baileys. It was a gourmet feast. But Mom barely touched it.

"Mom, what's wrong with the dinner?" I asked, the hurt breaking though my voice.

"I'm sorry, Carrie. It's a lovely dinner, but my teeth aren't strong enough for steak and everything is missing salt."

"But, Mom, you know you can't have salt,"

"I know, but I still miss it. I miss the foods we ate when your dad was with us," she added.

After I helped Mom into bed, it took me a long time to be ready for sleep. I sat in the room that had once been my bedroom. This was my special space from age ten to eighteen, when I left for college. I had shared the room with Maria for many of those years. It still bore the horrid lime green paint I used when Maria went off to college. I thought the green would make the room my own. Mostly, it just made it very green.

In the closet were still the dress I wore to prom and my bridesmaid dress from Maria's wedding. On the wall was the spot where I threw a shoe at Maria when she made fun of my first boyfriend.

Here is where I practiced my flute for hours. The desk where I did my homework was still in the corner. I suffered terrible fevers when I was young. Many nights Mom mopped my brow with a cool wash cloth. And here is where I was faking sleep as my dad lay dying. I remember the awful sound of death rattle that still rings in my ears. I was just sixteen.

I had a special bond with my father. One that I never quite shared with Mom. Dad and I loved baseball, especially the St. Louis Cardinals. I remember his last words to me, "See that the Cardinals win the World Series this year." They did. I've always suspected he had something to do with that.

It had been so long since I slept in here. My last night was the night before my wedding. I hadn't lived here for a number of years before I got married, but moved back in a couple of months before Geoff and I got married. We found a great apartment and Geoff had moved in, but I wouldn't share it with him until we were married. That was so long ago. Mom was nearly my age then. There were two more people in the world, Adam and Julie, nearly grown now. How quickly life had come full circle.

Now, I was the caregiver and Mom was the child. It was me that was doing the wash and cooking the meals. It was me that bathed her with a warm washcloth before she went to bed. It was me that helped her off with her clothes and on with a nightgown. It was me that was cleaning up her accidents. I just couldn't remember how we got here. How did all that time pass? How did life get so turned around? My cheeks were wet with tears as I fell asleep.

The next morning was Sunday. I made Mom a quick bowl of oatmeal before I left for church. From my earliest memories, attending church on Sunday was always a given. It was drilled into my very soul. My dad always said he'd rather lose his business than miss church. We were never open on Sunday mornings.

Our church made tapes of the services, so I got one for Mom. On the way home, I stopped at Walmart and got a tape player so Mom could hear the service. Then I stopped at the grocery store. No more fancy steaks for Mom. I learned my lesson. From now on, it would be food I grew up on. Food that was easy to chew. Catfish was one of our staples, so tonight we would eat catfish with sweet potatoes and slaw, just like when I was a kid.

It was nearly noon when I arrived back at Mom's. I came in with all my treasures, but couldn't find Mom. How could that be? She can hardly walk. She couldn't go very far. The oatmeal I had left for her was untouched. I started to panic. What if she had found her way out of the house? I would make one more turn around the house before I called Maria and the police.

Walking back into Mom's bedroom, I noticed the pile of blankets in the middle of the bed moving. I went over and uncovered Mom, rolled up in a ball.

"Mom," I cried, "what are you doing?"

"I'm hiding from the robbers in here," she said. "I thought if I curl up under these blankets, they won't see me."

Frightened, I asked, "You mean you had a dream about robbers?"

"Was that a dream?" she asked. "I thought there were robbers in the house."

"There are no robbers, Mom,"

"Did you check all over the house?" she asked in a very serious tone.

"Yes, Mom, I've checked, but if it makes you feel better, I'll look again."

I left for a walk around the house, not to search for robbers, but to pull myself together. I was clearing the house of bogeymen, not for a child, but for my mom.

Lord, help me, I prayed. *I'm not sure I can handle this.*

Once I convinced her the house was safe, I helped her dress and eat lunch. It was a lovely day, so I thought we might venture out. She had an old golf cart that she had used for years to help navigate the farm, so I took her for a ride on her trusty golf cart. We saw her beloved chickens, looked at the pear and apple trees full with fruit, and drove to the apple store. Maria came out to greet us. While Mom sat in the store for a while visiting with shoppers, I took Maria to the backroom and told her what had happened.

"I'm sure she just had a bad dream," Maria said in disbelief.

"No," I told her. "She had me searching the house for bogeymen. She thought it was real. I think this was some type of neurological episode. I think it's serious."

"But," Maria argued, "look at her! She's visiting with the customers just like the old days. There's nothing wrong. She's fine."

I knew she wasn't fine, but how could I argue? Mom looked great. The excursion outside did wonders for her. I was the only one who saw her in crazy mode. No one would believe me now.

We went back to the house and made the catfish dinner. I put a chair by the kitchen counter, and Mom showed me how to prepare the catfish. Of course, I knew how to prepare catfish, but it made her feel more involved helping. We fixed the sweet potatoes her way and made her famous slaw recipe. She ate everything, right down to the last crumb. John came in for his turn with Mom just as I finished the dishes. I was feeling very accomplished. I had made a dinner she loved.

I set up her tape player so she could hear the church service, and we had a lovely evening.

Before I left, I heard her say to John, "We had a lovely day. Maria took me for a ride and made me a catfish dinner."

I drove home with my heart in my stomach. I realized, no matter how hard I worked, even if I got everything right for Mom, she could never recognize me for what I did.

I was doing the right thing. Nothing else should matter. It was only my selfishness that wanted recognition. Still, I longed for her approval. I felt, once again, like the lost teenager, searching for affirmation and praise. Maybe that's what hurt most of all. I thought I had put that teenage self far behind me. I had worked for thirty years to become a confident woman. And yet, here she was again. It hurt more than words could express.

Chapter 6
Moving Forward

Monday morning, I went back to work. As people in the office were sharing about their weekends, I had little to say. Part of my silence was due to exhaustion. My weekend had been physically and mentally taxing, but nobody wanted to hear that, certainly nobody at my agency. When people asked me how my weekend was, I'd just say "Hard."

During the Monday morning staff meeting, I listened to people talking about concerts or movies or football games they had seen over the weekend. I just saw my mother. I didn't even see my husband all weekend. On the other hand, I did feel like I was connecting with my mother in a way I hadn't done in a very long time. I was learning things about her that I might have missed without this forced togetherness. But I couldn't turn off the caregiver and turn on the agency executive. I kept thinking, *Did Mom take her pills today? I wonder if John will find the soup I left for her. Will Maria remember that she has a home nurse visit tomorrow?*

"So, Carrie, tell us about the status of the new Goodman's marketing attack," boomed Mr. Ryan. "Carrie, are you with us? Too much fun over the weekend?"

You really are an ass, I thought. If you only knew how much fun it was cleaning up my mom's pee.

"Sorry, Sally Brinkman will be presenting our plans to Goodman's management today. She's pleased with everything, so I'm not expecting any problems," I added.

"Thank you, Carrie, for joining us, and thank you for that report," said Mr. Ryan. "Please keep us posted."

Sally's presentation did go well. The plans and budget were approved. This was a big boost to Ryan Advertising. We were headed for a flat year, and this new push for Goodman's put us in the growth column for the year. Of course, there were no bonuses or awards, or even thanks. But I did still have a job, and Mr. Ryan was easing up on my continued absences.

The week passed without an event. I spent another weekend at Mom's, pretty much like the last. The dirt and trash were piling up again, so the cleaning was getting more intense. But Mom was gradually improving. We worked hard to find nutritious low-sodium options for Mom. She complained about the lack of salt, but ate what we prepared.

I worked hard to spend time with Geoff and Adam during the week so my weekend absence was less notable. The third week, I arranged a couple of days off, so I could spend weekdays with Mom and the weekend at home.

Adam had a big Saturday night game, and Geoff and I had a great time watching our son shine on the court. I couldn't say life was back to normal, but we had created a new normal, and it was working, mostly.

As the month passed and Mom continued to improve, Maria called a family meeting. We all three agreed that Mom had improved enough that it was no longer necessary for twenty-four-hour care. We revamped our schedule to make sure somebody contacted Mom every day, and someone visited her every other day. However, she would still need a lot of help for daily necessities.

We were able to work out a division of chores pretty easily. John would handle home repairs and yard work, anything outside, and anything that required tools. Since Mom's house was over forty years old, that could be considerable. Maria would handle contact with the doctors and supervising medications. That was very tricky.

By now, Mom was taking over a dozen pills a day. Monitoring dosages nearly required a pharmaceutical degree. Maria also agreed to continue to help Mom with bathing and washing her hair, since neither John nor I could see ourselves doing that. What was left for me was the domestic stuff, cleaning and cooking. I agreed to spend Sundays with Mom and take care of the house. It was a good plan. We shared the work pretty evenly, and we each were responsible for something that fit our personalities and talents. We decided we would share doctor appointments. Mom had to have blood levels taken regularly and needed to see a full army of specialist on a regular basis. One thing we all agreed on: It was a good thing our parents had three children. There was no way one of us could handle all this.

Our only disagreement was professional home care. I wanted to hire a senior service to take care of some of these tasks. I did a little digging and was astonished at the cost. Still, I thought, divided three ways, it was doable. Maybe Mom had a few dollars to help? But it was not doable for John and Maria. Mom's meager savings was being eaten up by prescription medications and co-pays. Maria pointed out that we still didn't know what the future would bring, and we needed to keep our reserves for worst-case scenarios. That left us all in a very somber mood as we departed. We had to do this on our own as long as we could. None of us knew what the future would hold.

As Mom improved, my Sundays got harder. That certainly was not what I had expected. But when Mom was sick and weak, she had little to say about my cleaning efforts. However, when she was feeling better, she had a lot to say. She carefully scrutinized my trash bin, even emptying it and going through every item to make sure I didn't throw out something "important." Mom had always been a saver, but since her illness she moved from saver to extreme hoarder. She refused to allow me to throw out anything. She pulled from the trash empty store containers, candy wrappers, used envelopes, and broken everything.

I couldn't move anything, throw out anything, or vacuum anywhere without her excessive criticism.

One Sunday afternoon, I finally had had enough. I walked out the door and over to Maria's house, a short block away. She was watching a football game with her husband, and I marched in and sat down.

"How's Mom?" she asked with a knowing look.

"She's fine, if I don't kill her," I snapped.

"So, what has she done now?" Maria asked.

"She went through the trash again and took out everything I put in. She took out a soda cup from McDonald's. She already has a dozen McDonald's soda cups. She took out a food service tray from take-out at the grocery store. It was even cracked. She even took out an orange peel," I nearly shouted. "How can I clean if I can't throw anything out?" I asked. "She's so paranoid about me throwing her stuff away. She's accused me of throwing out her income tax papers, her favorite shirt, and the TV remote. I've had it. I can't go back there." The rage dissipating a bit as I screamed it out.

"I know. She calls me every time you leave with a list of stuff she thinks you threw away. I know things get lost because she sets them down and forgets where they are. Did you find any of her missing items?" Maria asked.

"Yeah. The remote was under a sofa cushion. Mom can't lift the cushion so she couldn't check. The shirt was in the wash—she forgot she had put it there. I cleaned it. The income tax papers, I have no idea. But I do know what tax papers look like, and I'm sure I didn't throw them out."

Maria reached over to a desk drawer and pulled out a stack of tax papers.

"Here are her income tax papers. I took them last Tuesday. I told her I was taking them. I want our accountant to look them over. She should have known where they were. I can't leave these with her because she'll lose them again," she said.

"She's going to keep saying I took them, isn't she?" I asked knowingly.

"Yep," said Maria. "I'm sorry. There's not much I can do. Do you want to go home? I can finish up supper for you. Where does she think you went?"

I held up my little bag of trash. "She thinks I'm taking the orange peel and potato peel to the chickens. I have a chicken roasting in the oven. I should finish dinner."

My anger was gone now.

"Here, let me take care of this garbage," Maria said kindly. "Go back and just do what you can. Forget the cleaning. Enjoy your dinner. This should be a good time to share with Mom. She can't help how she is."

"I know. I just lost it. I'm forty-five years old. I can't bear to be treated like I'm two."

"Think about Mom's point of view," Maria offered. "She's eighty-two and she's the mom, but we're taking care of her like she was a small child. That has to be difficult to the extreme."

"I know," I repeated. "This isn't easy for any of us."

I got back to Mom's house, and she was sitting in her comfy chair in the living room, snoozing. With her sleeping, it was a lot easier to finish cleaning. The house wasn't clean to my standards, but at least it was clean enough to pass health department minimums.

I finished dinner. I had made some of the old family favorites: roast chicken, sweet potatoes, asparagus, and blackberry cake made with berries from her freezer. She helped make the cake from her ancient recipe and thought it was as good as anything she had ever baked.

After supper was cleaned up and leftovers neatly wrapped for future meals, we sat and talked. I wanted to keep the conversation away from her complaints about my cleaning, so I came back to our favorite subject: history.

"Mom, you never told me how you met Dad."

She looked up with the biggest smile I'd seen in a very long time.

"Well, he was sort of always around," she began. "You see, your dad, Joseph"—my dad was never anything but Joseph, not Joe, not Joey, always Joseph—"and my dad, your grandpa, were old friends. They were closer in age than he and I, actually. Your dad was a wild child. His mom died when he was only nine, and he often ran over to his closest neighbor, my grandparent's house, and hung around my father and uncles. I guess my grandma was the closest person to a mother he knew.

"His family spoke mostly German, never English at home. My dad's family spoke both German and English, so he could talk to them. He had a lot of trouble with school because it was in English and he only knew German.

"Anyway, when my dad married my mom, Joseph kept up the friendship. He was a renowned scoundrel and Grandma didn't like him coming around much. He got your grandpa into plenty of trouble. They even got arrested once for building a still. I think Grandma told him he couldn't come around again after that. So, we didn't see much of him when I was little, but by the time I was a teenager, Grandma let up a bit and he started coming around again. He would help Grandpa out with the farming, and Grandpa would give him a little money or food. He'd stay and play with us kids. We'd go ice skating and fishing and picking whatever was ripe.

"Joseph was pretty down on his luck. In the winter he was a trapper. He would live in the Ozarks during the winter and hunt mink or fox or whatever he could sell for furs. He sold them in the spring to the fur companies in St. Louis, but he'd go through that money pretty fast and he'd come looking for work.

"I guess I was sixteen or seventeen when Grandpa let him live in the hay loft for working on the farm. Joseph learned everything he knew about growing things, especially fruit trees, from your grandpa. He didn't have much formal schooling, but he was a quick learner and he loved to see things grow.

"I guess I thought he was the most handsome man I had ever seen. He had a girlfriend, pretty serious for a while. But I guess she grew tired of him not earning enough money to get married, so she left. He was really sad and liked to talk to me. I could listen to him all night. My mom didn't like me talking to him so much, so I'd wait until my parents were asleep and sneak out of the house to talk with him."

She blushed so deeply she was beet red. I had never seen her blush, but then I'd never heard her talk so openly about my dad either.

"My mom was glad when I took the live-in maid job," Mom continued. "This way, I only saw Joseph on weekends, she thought."

There was that blush again.

"Truth is, I got him a job as a gardener for the Augustines. So, he worked three days a week for the Augustines and three days a week for my dad. I guess my mom never knew that."

"And you got married not long after that?" I asked.

"Yes, not long after that," she smiled. "I loved him so much. I could see what a good heart he had, even if my parents could not. We knew we couldn't bear to be apart. Marriage was the only solution."

There was a long pause in her story. So many thoughts were racing through my mind, I hardly noticed. Before long, I heard a steady breathing rhythm. Mom was sound asleep with the loveliest smile on her face. I could imagine that she was dreaming of a lovely young girl climbing into the hay loft in the dark of night for a forbidden tryst with this handsome rogue.

He was the man of her dreams, but he was all wrong. He had no education, no career plans, no money, and no family connections. Yet, here we are, decades later, so much the better for this illicit tryst between a pretty shy young girl and the handsome wandering gadfly.

There were 25 years of married bliss, or as close as most people ever come. There are three adults that would have never been without this meeting, not to mention our children and our children's children. And there is a significant business that bears his name. How many of the hundreds of people who pass through the Schmidt Farms' pumpkin patch or apple orchards know of the midnight tryst that set this all in motion?

I did know my grandparents strongly disapproved of my father. He was okay as a field worker, but never as a son-in-law. They were married for years before my grandparents acknowledged the union. Actually, it was not until Maria was born that they opened their door to my dad. But we never knew any of this as children. My mother always kept all unpleasantness away from us. I wonder what it cost her to forgive her parents and how many times she wanted to tell us, but never did. To us, she was always the loving, dutiful daughter to her parents.

Mom began to stir and it wakened me from my thoughts. I helped her into her nightgown and tucked her into bed, just like she had tucked me into bed in this very house hundreds of times. As I drove home, I said a little prayer thanking God for his divine plan, that the young girl named "Dorothy" and handsome, lost man named "Joseph" had found each other. I thanked God for my mother's illness that brought us together. If she had left for heaven when she had the first attack in her basement, we would have never had these wonderful talks. I would have lost the opportunity to really get to know her.

Yes, God, you do know best. God is good, all the time.

Chapter 7
Finding Balance

Thanksgiving came and went pretty uneventfully. I prepared the big Thanksgiving dinner at my house, much to my family's chagrin. They hated the hurry and bustle of preparation. They also hated how I turned into an angry drill sergeant when I was preparing a big meal for company. But we got through it.

Maria and John were almost an hour late. Her only duty was to bring Mom, but that turned into a major event. Even though we had discussed our plans with Mom several times, she was not ready, but trying to make a pie when Maria came to pick her up. Not only was there pie mess everywhere, Mom was nowhere near dressed. Maria had to find clean clothes, help Mom fix her remaining hair, and get teeth and hearing aids in place. Maria had to call in John to assist getting Mom ready and into and out of the car. We had not done that much over the past month, and it proved more difficult than expected. But once she got to my house, she was her warm, pleasant old self. We passed the day with many thanks for having our mom with us one more holiday.

Three days after Thanksgiving, Maria's daughter Katie gave birth to a handsome baby boy. They named him Joseph for my father, and there were tears and cheers all around. Katie was the perfect mother I always wished I had been. Her children were as dear to me as grandchildren could ever be.

I had a lovely visit with my daughter, Julie, home from college for a whole week. We shopped and dined and even got our nails done together. Adam had a basketball game the day after Thanksgiving, so we had a lovely family time together. Julie's graduation was coming up in the spring so we spent hours planning for her celebration. It was my hope that my sister and brother and mother would be able to make the six-hour drive to Northwestern University. It was a lot to ask.

On Sunday, Julie went back to college and I went to visit Mom. I made turkey soup, one of Mom's favorites, with the leftover turkey carcass. Mom instructed me as I chopped and cooked. She added stories from Thanksgivings past and many turkey soups from long-gone days. When we finished dinner, Mom wanted to talk about Christmas.

"It was so nice to see Julie," Mom said. "I don't get to see her or Adam very much. I want to have something nice to give them for Christmas, but I haven't got much money. I don't know how I will ever go shopping. I just can't make these old legs walk through a mall. Even if I could, bathrooms aren't handy enough for me. I might have an accident."

This was as close as Mom had come since her illness to demonstrating some understanding of her condition. Perhaps it was the holidays she loved so much that brought back her lucidity. I was touched beyond measure.

"You know, Mom, lots of people shop on the Internet these days. I bet we could go to the apple store and shop from their computer."

"Really, would you help me with that?" she asked excitedly. "I would like that."

"Absolutely. We'll do it next week."

"One more thing," she added. "I would like you to help me with a small Christmas tree. I know I can't have a big one like I usually do but just a little one would be nice. Oh, and could you help me get to church a couple of times during the Christmas season? I miss church. Oh, I guess that's two things, isn't it?" She smiled.

I had to look away so she didn't see the tears. Of course, I would do all these things. The possibility that this was her last Christmas loomed large. I wondered if she knew this too.

"Yes, Mom, I'll take care of it," I said.

I had much to think about as I drove home with tears rolling down my face.

Work was ramping up for the holidays. It always happens this time of year. Some client has remaining marketing funds that must be spent before the end of the year. If they don't spend all their allocated funds, next year's budget will be cut. There are multiple little projects to be created, managed, produced, and invoiced before December 30. I was working through lunch and sometimes dinner, too. The whole agency was in chaos. And then there was the holiday entertaining. Clients expected to be taken to liquid Christmas lunches or dinners, which was more of a chore for me than the end-of-the-year projects.

I love everything about the holidays: the carols, the decorating, the shopping, the wrapping, the baking, the heartwarming Christmas services. But I didn't have a clue how I would find the time to do it all. In addition, each of my kids had special events that couldn't be missed. Adam had endless basketball games, and Julie was coming home for the holidays expecting me to spend lots of quality time discussing her future, planning for graduation, and shopping.

By this time, Mom was mobile enough to get to the doctor, or at least so the insurance company determined. This meant we could no longer get home visits paid by insurance, so Maria, John, and I had to find a way to get Mom through the gauntlet of doctors.

Each organ of Mom's body had its own doctor: cardiologist, neurologist, urologist, gynecologist, optometrist, dermatologist, podiatrist, and dentist. Everything was failing and in need of repair. I actually think we could take Mom to a different doctor every day of the week. As it was, we managed the most urgent needs and hoped for the best with the rest. Maria took Mom to the cardiologist, who was managing her medications and needed to take regular blood levels. I took Mom to the urologist because she was having urinary tract troubles, possibly caused by the medications prescribed by the cardiologist. John took Mom to the physical therapist, who could also no longer make home visits on insurance. Physical therapy was prescribed by the cardiologist to help her get more mobile.

Each trip out required us to call her multiple times to remind her of the appointment, then we had to arrive nearly an hour early because she would invariably not be ready. Getting Mom ready for a doctor visit required finding clean clothes, inserting hearing aids, and getting her false teeth in place—and making sure she made a bathroom visit. Before leaving we would have to locate her insurance card, her checkbook, her purse, scarf, and coat.

I'd pull my car up to her front porch through the lawn so Mom would have the least number of steps from house to car. Getting into the car was difficult to the extreme. Once I had Mom in the car, I'd load her walker and cane in the trunk.

When we got to the doctor, we would have to reverse the process: get the walker out of the trunk and Mom in the door and find a place for her to sit while I parked the car. I'd run back in before Mom decided to try to find her own way up the elevator to the doctor's office or some *thoughtful* person decided to help and I'd lose her.

I thought it would be easier when we were finally in the doctor's office until the nurse said she'd need a urine sample and handed Mom a cup. The idea of this eighty-two-year-old lady, who could hardly use the toilet herself and missed it most of the time, managing to actually get urine in a cup was so ludicrous I just burst out laughing. The nurse was not amused. She gave me an incriminating look, put the cup back and held up a "hat" that fit over the whole toilet seat. Still chuckling despite my best efforts to stop, I shook my head in agreement and lead Mom to the bathroom. The rest of the visit went fairly normal.

Before I could go in with my mom, the nurse had to ask her if it was okay that this person—me—could come into the exam room. Mom looked puzzled. The nurse muttered something about privacy laws and we went in. No one noticed that I was holding my breath. I was terrified that Mom would say no.

No one knew what would come out of her mouth next. If I didn't go in, the doctor would surely get incorrect information and whatever the doctor told Mom would be lost. She could hardly remember having a doctor visit, much less what he said. But I couldn't argue the point. What was I supposed to say? *Hey guys, she's half crazy. Why are you asking her?* Not only would that get me nowhere, it would hurt Mom's feelings. Whoever proposed the privacy laws surely doesn't have aging parents. Fortunately, she said yes, so I could enter.

The doctor discussed why she was having frequent urinary tract infections, which I'm sure went right over her head. Then he said, "We should see you back next month."

I want to shout, *No, please no*, but I said, "Is it necessary? I have to take a day off work to get her here," I pleaded.

Mom caught that too well and said, "I'm sure Maria will be glad to bring me."

Now, the thing I was trying so hard to avoid was out. I made a great effort to hide from Mom my frustration and anxiety over losing a day's work. I didn't want her to think my work was more important than her. I didn't want to think that either, but there it was, always under the surface, in the deep dark places of my ambition.

I had taken a half day off, left at noon, and didn't plan to return to work. My boss would never understand this.

Shopping with Mom on the Internet didn't work out too well. Visualizing an item in one dimension just wasn't working for her, so I thought we would try the old fashion way. I knew Mom wanted to go to Penney's so I thought we would start there. I told Mom the mall had wheelchairs we could borrow, but she was so negative on that idea that I quickly let it drop. Even with Mom's handicap parking pass, we couldn't get close enough to the store, so I pulled right in front, got the walker from my trunk, and helped her in the store. It would have worked well if the store had any place to sit, but there was nothing.

I told Mom to go on in the store and I'd catch up with her. By the time I had parked and caught up, she had already found two items she wanted: one for Maria and one for Katie. She next wanted to buy John a pair of shoes, so I helped her to the shoe department and she quickly found a pair of work shoes that she wanted. I made sure we had all the receipts tucked neatly in her purse. She wanted to find a new blouse for Christmas, so we made our way to an elevator and up to the next floor. She walked a small way and suddenly stopped.

"I don't think I can go any further," Mom said. "I'm just worn out."

I knew this was a stretch, but I was hopeful. I asked the sales lady if there were any chairs in the store. To my surprise, she found a folding chair from the storeroom and brought it out for Mom. While Mom rested comfortably—more or less—in the chair, I brought her several styles and colors of shirts. She picked one and I purchased it for her.

"We could go to another store if you would let me get a wheelchair," I offered.

"No," she said firmly. "It's not time for a wheelchair yet. I'll get Maria to take me another day. I think I need to go home."

On the way home, we passed our favorite soft-serve ice cream store.

"How about an ice cream cone?" I asked.

"That sounds lovely," Mom said. We could always agree on ice cream. We had a wonderful time eating our ice cream. I suppose I inherited my passion for the stuff from Mom. With the happy ice-cream high, we parted cheerfully. I carried all her purchases to her bedroom as directed and promised to return to help with Christmas decoration.

The next great challenge was getting Mom to church. It was decided the late service the Sunday before Christmas would be the best time for Mom. This request, however, was going to take a village. The difficulty for Maria and me was that we were busy with Sunday School. The problem for John was that it was Sunday and church. He seemed to have an aversion to getting out of bed at all on Sunday, his only day off; and going to church was definitely not on his to-do list, ever.

We devised a plan that Maria would stop in and wake Mom up, lay out her church clothes, and head off to Sunday School. Geoff would come by an hour later and bring Mom up to church just as Sunday School was over. I would meet Geoff at the door, help Mom to a seat, and bring her home after service.

When Geoff got to Mom's house, she was not nearly ready. I should have warned him of this, but forgot. Mom couldn't get on her pantyhose and Geoff had to help. There is no amount of favors I could ever do to pay Geoff back for this if we lived another hundred years. I can't imagine that Mom was too pleased either, but she was happy to be at church.

They forgot her hearing aids, so I don't think she heard much, but she loved the songs. When time came to take communion, the usher bent over and offered to bring the host and wine to Mom. She flatly refused and insisted on finding her way up to the altar with the rest of the congregation. This seemed like ultimate stubbornness to me, but I obediently helped her unfold the walker and make her way to the front of the church at her own pace.

The church was resplendent with shimmering Christmas trees and elegant garland. Extra candles burned everywhere and poinsettias from Schmidt Farms graced the altar.

As I followed Mom to the altar, I was suddenly struck by how old she looked. In my mind, Mom will forever be the handsome forty-three-year-old widow of my youth, but now she was bent and broken. Her thinning hair was poorly styled and white as snow. Her clothes were neat, but hung awkwardly on her bent frame. She was so frail, yet so determined. I was filled with so many emotions: sorrow at seeing my mother's decline, but joy that she was still with us. Memories of so many trips to communion filled my mind.

As I took the host from our pastor, tears were rolling down my face. Pastor Mueller reached out and gently touched my arm. It was a beautiful gesture, but it had the opposite result he intended. It opened the flood gate for the tears. I walked back to our seat with tears now streaming down my face. I looked out at the congregation and wondered what they thought of the bent, frail, old lady walking in front of me. How many remembered her younger days? How many knew her years of service to the church? How sad it was that so many people only knew the bent, old lady and not the vibrant mother of three children that led a business to success. She had preserved so much in life.

The last days before Christmas were crazy. I just couldn't fit everything into twenty-four-hour days. I was trying to spend as much time as possible with Julie, which meant less time with Mom. John agreed to wrap Mom's presents, which was a great gesture, but he got several of them mixed up. I suggested she just put a check in cards, but she would have none of that. There must be a wrapped gift for each grandchild, great grandchild, and each of her siblings. That meant a lot of scurrying around the last few days.

Presents bought weeks ago went missing. Searching for the lost presents, we actually found some that she had purchased last year. As Christmas approached, Mom was more and more unhappy with the little tree I had installed in her living room and convinced John to go and get her a *real* tree. He did a fine job of setting up the tree, but left unpacked boxes everywhere. To top it all off, when all the presents were unwrapped on Christmas, I realized that I had not received a present from Mom. After all the work I did making sure everybody on the list had a gift, mine somehow had fallen through the crack.

Maria noticed my forlorn look and guessed the reason.

"Did we lose your gift from Mom?" she said kindly.

I know it wasn't lost. I was just forgotten.

"I'm sure we will find it when everything's cleaned up," she offered.

"That's okay," I lied. "It doesn't really matter."

But, of course it did. Not only was I sad about being forgotten, I was now feeling embarrassed for being sad.

By the time Christmas was over, we were fully exhausted and totally missing the reason for the season.

My Christmas joy smashed, I limped through the remaining holidays. Julie was happy to return to the sanity of school, and I to work.

Two weeks into the New Year, I spent a Sunday at Mom's cleaning up her Christmas mess. It took every bit of five hours to take down the now dried tree John had erected, pack away her ornaments, and clean up the debris left behind by wrapping and baking. For the first time in memory, I was happy to see the holidays end.

Chapter 8
A New Year

The New Year brought with it a new normal. While we were deep into the winter months, Maria and John had more time to spend with Mom, and I had more time to spend with my family and less time to spend at work. The big program we had completed for Goodman's was moderately successful, which was enough for Sally and Mr. Goodman, but not for Mr. Ryan. It didn't quite meet his grand expectation. But more importantly, it failed to win the coveted Arch Advertising Award at the Advertising Club banquet. That was unforgivable. I never quite understood the importance put on these awards, but it meant everything to Mr. Ryan. In his strange view, no award meant no success.

"So, Carrie, do you have the new marketing plan in place for Goodman's?" he asked. "And does *this* plan include an Arch Advertising Award for my wall?"

"As we've discussed," I replied, "this year's marketing plan for Goodman's is a little austere. We overspent their budget last year, so they are spending a little less this year. And as I have no control over the voting for the Arch Advertising Awards, no, we probably won't be getting one of those either."

The words shot from my mouth before I knew I had said them.

"Well," said Mr. Ryan without missing a beat, "I suggest you find a new client as soon as possible to make up for the income we have now lost from Goodman's. And make it a client that *will* win us an award."

Sam was first to speak to me after the meeting broke up.

"Is this a new Carrie?" he asked. I could only look puzzled. "One that answers back to the big boss," he smirked.

"No," Jamie quickly answered, "she's just showing her true colors."

She quickly turned her back on me and walked back to her desk. But Sam lingered, as if I was supposed to respond to his comment.

This was a revolting turn of events. In spite of our best efforts, and a certain amount of success, our business with Goodman's was reduced. The only two things I'm sure of is that I don't fit in this place and I don't have the time or energy to find a new job. Of course, the other two things I was sure of was that Julie was finishing four years of college, which we would be paying on for some time; and Adam would be off to college before Julie's education was paid. That meant this job was vital and I had to find a way to make it work.

I spent the rest of the winter searching hard for a new account. I made presentation after presentation. I signed a new project here or there, but not significant *award-winning* accounts.

I did continue my Sunday dinners with Mom. This had now become less a chore and more a staple in my life. I was never comfortable with the time it took from Geoff and Adam, but I was committed. I also discovered the thing that made Mom most happy was to cook, together, something she had often made. Catfish was one of our favorites. John often joined us for the catfish dinners. He was not a bad cook for a bachelor, but he didn't tackle fish. I generally made a pie, one of Mom's favorite foods. Sometimes I'd find berries carefully preserved in her basement freezer and make a dessert from the frozen fruit.

One snowy Sunday in late February, I was waiting for a blackberry buckle to cook and sat with Mom on the sofa. "You haven't told me yet about your wedding."

A broad smile came over her face, "Our wedding," she smiled. "Well, as you can imagine, my parents were furious when they found out that Joseph and I were dating. My dad threatened to shoot Joseph if he came near me again. We tried to stay apart, but just couldn't. Joseph decided if we were married, my parents would accept us. He was thirty-three and I was only eighteen. That never mattered to us, but I guess it did to other people. We were in love, and nothing else mattered.

"We saved for a couple of months until we had managed to pull together fifty dollars. That was just enough for two rings, a couple of nights at a little hotel in the Ozarks, and a Justice of the Peace to marry us. I bought this lovely navy dress with a dainty white-lace collar. Joseph had his church suit. My dress doesn't show up well in the photo, though."

She held up the wedding photo from off the coffee table. That photo was an indelible part of my childhood, but I never bothered to ask about the back story.

"It really was a lovely dress," she added a little mournfully.

"Your dad convinced two of his friends to join us to be our witnesses. They had to be his friends, because anybody I knew would tell my parents and that would be the end of it. I didn't know them well, but we had a lovely time. They were so kind to me and completely void of judgment. That was a big relief, since I had never been anywhere. It was all like a dream to me. But it quickly turned into a nightmare when we got back.

"The first thing we did was go directly to my parents. Joseph showed them the rings and documents. My dad got right up from the table and went to the backroom. He came out with his hunting rifle and shoved it in Joseph's face. 'I won't kill you because you're married, but I don't ever want to see either of you here again or I may not be so reasonable.' We were stunned.

"Then my dad turned to me and said, 'If you come to your senses and repent, we will take you back, but we won't ever see him again.' Then he walked out the door and went to his barn.

"My mother never said a word. She, too, walked out of the room. I left there in tears and didn't see my parents again for seven years. It was only after Maria was born that my parents forgave us."

"But," I said, stunned, "we never knew any of this. You loved your parents and I always thought they loved Dad."

"That's what forgiveness is," Mom answered. "When we reunited, it was like none of it ever happened. We had a new baby and they had a granddaughter. My dad and Joseph picked up their friendship like nothing ever happened. It didn't happen overnight, but gradually. We are all Christians. We know about forgiveness."

Yes, I thought, we should know about forgiveness, but even the most devout Christian would find it hard to forgive this. That was a big leap. I wondered if I could ever leap that far.

It had never occurred to me why the story of our parents' wedding was never told. After all, it was only one of many stories that were untold. Mom and Dad didn't discuss their history much, so it didn't seem unusual. By the time I was old enough to be interested in the story, Dad was gone and I assumed it was just too hard for Mom to talk about anything related to him. She didn't talk about anything that might cause her or us to be sad. That pretty much eliminated anything to do with Dad.

Dinner was lovely. Mom ate like it was her last meal. She praised everything I made and enjoyed it thoroughly. After the dishes were done, I tucked her into bed and kissed her good night, just as she had done when I was little. I gathered up all my cooking tools and packed them back in the car. As I walked to the car, the snow was falling fast and heavy. It was a fairly warm day and the snow wasn't sticking to the roads, but it was sticking to the trees and grass. It was just enough to blanket the farm with a beautiful coat of white.

I closed the trunk and stood for a moment in the cold, wet snow. As it floated around me, it brought back so many memories of happy snow days. The hill beyond the house, now wearing a blanket of white, is where my dad nearly broke his leg trying to stop the toboggan. We had hours of snow-day fun on that hill as children. The flat spot on the front yard is where we had built our snowmen. I remembered my mother running from the kitchen with apples and carrots to decorate our snow creatures. I can still see her removing her own scarf so I wouldn't worry about the snowman getting cold.

Tears were starting to freeze to my face when I finally returned to reality and drove home, eyes still wet with tears and memories of childhood past flooding though my mind.

My greatest struggle on these busy Sunday's was cleaning. It made the day long and very difficult. Mom was so suspicious of my cleaning. She had convinced herself, in her distorted mind, that I was throwing out important stuff. I had stopped announcing my visits in advance because it caused a storm of anxiety for Mom, worrying about what I might throw out in my cleaning. No amount of reasoning could allay her anxiety.

I felt we needed to find a better solution to cleaning her house, so I decided to call a family meeting to discuss Mom's care. Maria, forever seeing only rainbows, didn't think there was any problem. John was totally indifferent. His comment was, "She doesn't care about the dirt and clutter, why should we?"

Maria brought reason to the discussion. "Even if you don't care about the filth in Mom's house, we don't want our mother living like that. Just because she can't understand the need for cleaning, doesn't mean it shouldn't be done."

John just shrugged. He could always argue with me, but not Maria.

"What about a senior home service?" I asked.

"Where do you think the money for that is going to come from?" John snapped.

"Mom is not totally without funds," Maria quickly offered.

"We don't need somebody every day," I piped in. "If we just had someone who could come in and do some things for Mom a couple times a week, that would help."

"What do you think a senior helper would do?" John asked.

"I'm thinking light cleaning, most of what I do on Sundays. Dishes, maybe make a meal, see that Mom takes her meds, help her with her physical therapy exercises, and give Mom a bath."

"I'd go along with the cleaning and dishes, but Mom won't want anyone else to give her a bath," Maria said firmly. "Her bath is my chore and I like doing it for her."

"I get that, but how does your weak back and aching knees feel about it?"

I was truly concerned about Maria injuring herself bathing Mom.

"I'll manage," she replied. "Bathing Mom is not on the agenda."

The discussion was over.

"Okay, we'll search for someone who can do light housework, help Mom exercise, and give Mom meds." I concluded. It was agreed.

Over the next few days, I spoke with a half dozen firms who could provide the needed services. A couple of them were out of our price range; one wouldn't go so far in the country as Mom's house; and one was unresponsive. Maria made appointments with both of the selected firms. A clear winner was chosen from her interviews and a schedule established. I thought we had entered a new era of diminishing responsibilities. My optimism proved to be premature.

The caregiver that was sent to Mom was not a country person. She was repulsed by the food scraps Mom saved for the chicken, sickened by the strange concoctions Mom made for the birds, and refused to clean up all Mom's messes. She couldn't help Mom with her exercises because Mom "wouldn't do a thing," she said, including taking her meds. The meals she made for Mom were too strange and Mom refused to eat them. In short, in the one month we tried the caregiver, we paid half of our combined salaries for services Mom refused. The caregiver was so unhappy she refused to come back, even if we did want her. Mom was so miserable about the whole experiment that she would not even discuss alternatives.

Neither Mom nor Maria nor John would even discuss alternatives outside the home. Mom had attached herself to that house like Gorilla Glue and nothing short of complete loss of mind and body would pry her from it.

Chapter 9

Finding a New Way

After months of searching for a new major client, I finally hit on a promising prospect. Bobby Wright was an infamous local entrepreneur I had worked with about five years ago. At that time, he had owned a national grocery supply company. We lost Mr. Wright as a client when he sold the company at a handsome profit due, at least in part, to our brilliant advertising campaign. I always thought we got the short end of the stick. However, Mr. Wright had not forgotten us. He was ready to buy a new company and wanted Ryan Advertising and me to help him make a success of this company too.

In March, he called me to discuss his new venture. He had found a company that sold office supplies and wanted to know if we could help him make this company compete with the likes of Staples and Office Depot.

Mr. Ryan started the staff meeting with his usual review of current projects and then took a deep breath to start on his latest rant. I interrupted before he had a chance to say a word.

"I think I have found us a new client," I started.

Matt Ryan is not one to be out-staged.

"Another flower shop, I assume," he jeered.

"I wouldn't call Bobby Wright's new business a flower shop," I smirked back.

"You bagged Bobby Wright?" exclaimed Sam, who, for some odd reason, was now firmly ensconced in my camp.

"I sure did," I bragged. "And his new company is bigger than Goodman's," I proudly proclaimed.

There were so many things wrong with this proclamation I hardly knew where to start. I didn't actually have a contract yet with Mr. Wright. I knew that before the "bag" would be closed, I would need the help of everybody in the agency. Somewhere between my anger and Mr. Ryan's attitude, I had succumbed to the dark side. But this wasn't me, and I'm no good at these games. Still, I needed this account. After all, I had another four years of college to pay for. There was no retreat now.

"I'll have this wrapped up by the end of the week."

What was even more miraculous, I did. Funny thing about success... It makes you forget where all blessings come from. It made me prideful and cocky.

I was in my most creative zone, developing new ideas for logos, slogans, and ads, working late every night and enjoying every minute. Both Geoff and Adam thought I had completely forgotten them. Maybe I had. The only thing that kept me grounded was my Sundays with Mom. It's hard to be too cocky when you're cleaning up pee on your mother's bathroom floor and scraping moldy food from forgotten plates.

Each week I would bring Mom special dishes I had made at home for her to eat during the week. Some weeks I would find the empty dishes sitting in the sink, where they had been for days; sometimes I would find the lovingly prepared dishes still in the fridge, rotting. Or I would find traces of Mom's attempts to cook: burnt pans, dried-up spilled eggs, and rotting, half-peeled veggies. Mom might pour herself a glass of milk and forget it, until I found it curdled on Sunday. As difficult as cleaning these messes was, I was more worried that she wasn't getting sufficient nutrition.

John and Maria were spending all their free time escorting Mom around town to her various doctors and therapy appointments. They left the mess for me. It was only fair, but it didn't feel very fair to me. With my new interest in work, I was avoiding the doctor appointments as much as possible. I tried to revisit the idea of finding an assisted-living arrangement, but neither Mom nor Maria would discuss it. I suggested maybe Mom should move in with Maria, but got a very definitive no from both parties. We were all stuck. Mom was stuck like glue to her house, and we were stuck with doing the best we could to take care of her there.

The bright side was that May was fast approaching, and we were all preparing to head to Chicago for Julie's college graduation. Not that we needed any more excitement, but Julie announced that her new boyfriend and his mother would join us. Julie had never introduced us to a boyfriend before, much less a boyfriend's family. Mom was determined to go, and Maria was certain she and her husband, Bill, could manage getting her there for a two-day trip. John was happy to stay home and watch the store.

We knew Mom could never manage the extensive walking required to attend the graduation events, so we rented a wheelchair. She was resolved that the wheelchair was necessary, but would only commit to a rented one. She was determined to go and nothing could dissuade her. She wanted everything to be perfect. She even asked me to take her shopping for a new dress. I was touched that Julie meant so much to her, but I'm not sure it wasn't more the idea of a road trip. It had been years since Mom left the confines of St. Louis County. I think the idea of the freedom of travel, one more time, was irresistible.

May came quickly. Mom's spirits were up with anticipation. A graduation tends to do that. It represents the success of another child. You can finally exhale because you managed to guide your child through the rough spots, out of those terrible teens, and into adulthood with a diploma in hand. That diploma is a pronouncement to the world that you succeeded as a parent, and all near relatives are eager to share the success and join in with congratulations. The graduation had a little extra excitement because we were meeting a serious boyfriend and his family. My mother applauded the potential *Mrs. degree* every bit as much as the bachelor's degree.

Julie presented us with another surprise a month before graduation. She had a full scholarship from Northwestern to stay and get her master's degree, which she accepted. It may have been the reluctance to leave Chicago and her new boyfriend that encouraged her to stay; but in any case, it seemed a big honor, and we were bursting at the already tight seams from pride.

I'll have to admit that I was a little sad Julie would not be coming home. She had an internship for the summer and would start her master's program immediately. I had been looking forward to spending more time with her doing some of the things we used to do, but she was on a different path and I was happy for her.

The day came for us to head toward Chicago, and I was so nervous, you'd think I was graduating. I had forgotten my camera, which I discovered before we reached the highway and we went back to pick it up. We bought drive-through breakfast off the interstate, which I nearly threw up from nerves. Adam was oblivious to the excitement. Mostly, it meant some free meals and a couple days out of school. But he wasn't quite sure it was worth the boredom. I had to wonder, as I watched him reading his WWF magazine in the back seat, if this day would ever come for him. I suggested he might try a classic novel to help shore up his English.

He just mumbled, "It's never happening."

We had a long schedule of restaurant reservations three nights in a row. The first night was a local favorite upscale sports bar. This was our big opportunity to meet Julie's boyfriend, Paul.

Paul was the answer to every mother's prayer. He had a perfect boyfriend resume: good education, good job, good health, and church member. I had to take a moment and offer a prayer of thanks that God had guided Julie well. Paul fit into our family extremely well. Even Adam liked him, although he felt Paul was a little on the nerdy side. That was just fine with Geoff and me.

Maria, Bill, and Mom came the next day, just in time for dinner. They had a little trouble finding the hotel and getting Mom from the lobby to the room. We got a great rate at a discount hotel, but the extra amenities were lacking. We had requested a handicap room for Mom, but I couldn't see any handicap facilities except a bar on the bathtub.

Mom was exhausted and it took her a long time to get ready for dinner. Geoff, Adam, Julie, and I went on to the restaurant to hold the reservation. A table for eight isn't easy to get anywhere near Chicago. I knew Mom had arrived when we heard a great commotion at the front of the restaurant.

Maria and Bill had trouble getting Mom and the wheelchair in the door, partly because she kept trying to get out of the wheelchair. Once they were in, Mom thought she should walk to the table, so there was more conflict. They finally convinced her to let them push her to the table where she could transfer to a chair. All this made the introductions to Paul a little awkward, but we worked our way through it and had a lovely dinner even though Mom complained it was too expensive.

The next day was graduation. It started at ten o'clock, which meant an early morning. We all met for a quick breakfast, although nothing with a group that size is ever quick. We wanted to get to the arena where the graduation was held early enough to find a good spot. As soon as we managed to swallow a little breakfast, we headed out. We were only a mile from the basketball stadium where the ceremony was to be held. Knowing parking would be impossible, we thought we'd walk.

We didn't know very much about wheelchairs, which became painfully obvious when we headed down the street. The rented chair had very little cushion for Mom and she bounced around, comically, as we pushed her over the uneven sidewalk.

Julie and Paul left earlier, so our group included Maria, Bill, Adam, Geoff, me, and Mom, in the feeble rented wheelchair. Geoff and Bill took turns pushing Mom. That's another thing we didn't know about wheelchairs. Some push harder than others. The one we had picked was a little like pushing a concrete truck. On top of that, the streets of Chicago are not wheelchair-friendly. They have potholes the size of Rhode Island that could completely swallow up a wheelchair, including the person inside and the person pushing. We were walking fast because we were a little late.

I had just made it through a stoplight and turned around to see Geoff pushing Mom as hard as he could to get through the stoplight. Suddenly, he smashed into a huge pothole. The wheelchair dropped into the pothole with such a force you could hear the crunch a mile away. Geoff nearly collapsed on top of the chair as his momentum forced him forward. Mom flew in air from the impact and then down again into the chair. It all seemed to happen in slow motion. But there they were, firmly stuck in a pothole in the middle of a busy intersection with cars buzzing around them. Fortunately, some very kind drivers—probably tourists—stopped to give us a chance to extricate the wheelchair from the pothole. Adam and I ran into the street and helped lift the chair out and to the sidewalk. Once on safe ground, we took a deep breath.

I don't know if it was the trauma or excitement, but I just started to laugh. I was nearly doubled over laughing when Geoff pointed out the time. Mom was laughing, too, for which I was very thankful. I managed to pull myself together enough to continue walking. We got to the stadium and found our seats without any additional drama. The ceremony was beautiful. I cried. Maria cried. Mom smiled.

That evening we had a lovely party at a local Italian restaurant. We ordered family style. Julie opened graduation presents. We all enjoyed meeting Paul's mom. They fit in like we had known them for years. I could see a bright future for Julie and it gave me peace. For one glorious evening, the world was perfect. I sat watching all the people I loved, together, enjoying a special moment and thought the world was perfect.

I will never lose the image of Mom, in that feeble wheelchair, stuck in the middle of a busy Chicago street with Geoff terrified behind her. She never mentioned the horror of that near-fateful walk to the stadium. She never complained. Maybe that is why she was so determined to go. Perhaps she knew that and wanted to leave her grandchildren a fun memory. I'll never know, but the first thing we did when we got home was find Mom a proper wheelchair.

Chapter 10

My Perfect World, Crumbling

Funny thing about those perfect moments in life: They never seem to last. Maria said Mom was very jovial all the way home. She loved watching farms go past from the car, but the trip took a toll on her. She found it hard to get out of bed for the next week. We assumed she was just exhausted from the trip and she would be better after resting for a while. She never complained of any other symptoms, so we continued checking in on her from time to time and going about our business.

Even with my success on landing Bobby Wright's new venture, Ryan Advertising had hit a rough patch. With the economy slumping, many of our accounts had either vanished or reduced their advertising spending. That always meant bad news for the agency. I had hoped that Office and More, the new name we had picked for Mr. Wright's office supply company, would fill in the void. The project was going well, but it took time.

Before we could create any advertising, we had to do extensive research on the market, competition, and the business model of the new company. With that in place, we had to find a new name and logo. Meanwhile, the agency was losing money. Mr. Ryan was less annoying now, but much more sullen. He stopped berating people, but he was now sulking around the office in a fashion that left us all with an impending-doom feeling.

We were all trying. I was still working way past closing time. I conducted or supervised all the research and wrote any necessary copy.

We had scheduled a major presentation of the new logo, and I was working hard on the presentation. Sam was working hard on the design too. We often found ourselves working long after everyone else had left.

One evening a couple of weeks after I returned from Julie's graduation, I was about to call it quits for the day at the same time Sam was closing his computer. He walked over to my desk and asked if I'd like to have a drink to celebrate our success. It sounded like a nice idea, but it was not the kind of thing I did very often. I did, however, need a friend at work.

We went to quiet little pub near the office and had a nice time talking about our families. Sam was divorced, for the second time. He loved talking about how awful both wives were. I had to wonder if some of that wasn't Sam, but it felt good to have someone confide in me. I shared some problems with Geoff, too, most of which were as much my fault as his; but it felt good to sound like the *victim*. When I got home, I didn't want to talk to Geoff at all. I was feeling guilty about speaking badly of him to Sam, so I just climbed into bed and pretended to go to sleep.

A couple of days later, Sam and I made the big presentation to the Office and More employees. I don't think they were thrilled with the idea of being bought by Bobbie Wright, but they were welcoming to us and trying to make the best of the changes we presented. Bobbie, on the other hand, was thrilled and made a big show of his appreciation. Sam and I were feeling full of success as we drove back to the office. Sam suggested we ditch work and stop for drinks and an early dinner. It sounded like fun, so I agreed. It was so nice to be appreciated by someone who was so totally unobligated to do so. It had been a very long time since someone unrelated to me showed any interest at all in me. Sam's new attention to me was very flattering.

It was late when we headed back to the car. Night had fallen. We had arrived there in Sam's car. He was going to drive me back to the office. He walked me to the passenger side of the car and reached to open the door, but then turned and kissed me on the cheek. I turned to face him and he kissed me full on the mouth. For a second, I kissed him back. This kind of thing didn't happen to me. This kind of thing couldn't happen to me.

As suddenly as it happened, I realized what I was doing. I was not only betraying my devoted husband, but everything I believed. This wasn't me at all.

I jumped back from Sam and said, "Sam, I'm sorry if I gave you a wrong impression, but I'm married."

"I know that," Sam replied. "So was I, twice."

"Well, I don't intend to be married twice," I snapped. "I'm going to go back in the restaurant and ask them to call me a cab." I turned to walk away.

"You don't need to do that," he shouted after me.

"Oh, yes, I do," I shouted back. I wasn't getting into his car. I had finally come to my senses and remembered who I was. I was more ashamed of myself at that moment than I had ever been.

In the cab riding back to the agency, I thought of all the times Sam had been so nice to me in the past few months. Had this been a plan of his? Did I give him any encouragement? Could he really think I would betray my husband? I vowed to make it up to Geoff.

For the next month, I was home on time every night and made all Geoff's favorites. I couldn't tell him, but I spent a lot of time asking God to forgive me. I wasn't sure Geoff would forgive, but I knew God would.

After my little adventure with Sam, things at work got very strange. I was cold to Sam because I wanted to make sure I wasn't passing any wrong signals. Our working relationship was strained and it showed. I don't know if anyone in the office noticed, but it seemed everyone was cold to me, especially Jamie.

I'm sure the strain on the agency from slow business didn't help matters. Things weren't picking up. In fact, Office and More was the only bright spot. Perhaps Mr. Ryan and everyone else resented me for that. In any case, Jamie was trying to derail me at every opportunity. She would open my mail and temporarily lose some of it. She misplaced phone notices. She took forever to finish clerical projects I had given her, even though I was the only one with work for her to do. I was missing a couple of things from my desk too. I couldn't confront her because I knew that's what she wanted. I had to be very careful with my things and hide anything she might take. I felt like I was at war all the time.

One warm June day, I was enjoying my lunch salad on the little patio in back of our office. I had completely given up trying to lunch with anyone in the office. I hated going to a restaurant by myself, so I usually ate at my desk or on the patio if weather permitted. I loved the quiet time, especially on warm sunny days. I stretched out and imagined I was anywhere else. I'm sure the rest of the office thought I was odd, eating alone like that, but it was the best I could do. I had just taken two bites when Jamie poked her head out the door and said, "I'm leaving. You need to watch the phones."

"But I'm just starting my lunch," I barked back. "You're not scheduled to leave for thirty minutes."

"Suit yourself," she replied matter-of-factly. "I'm leaving."

"No, you're not," I snapped. "You'll leave when I finish lunch," I shouted.

When I looked up, the whole office was watching.

She turned and looked at them. "Didn't I tell you what a bitch she was," she said softly. Then turned back to me and smiled. However, to the rest of the office, she said, tearfully, "She wants me to miss my nieces' birth."

George spoke up first. "We'll all cover for you Jamie, even if *she* won't."

I was caught in a well-planned trap.

"I'm terribly sorry, Jamie. I'll watch the phones for you."

"Don't bother," Sam piped up. "Stay out there."

That was the first I had heard from Sam since our uncomfortable encounter. I had no idea he was resentful.

As Jamie walked to the parking lot, she turned again and smiled.

I called Mr. Wright and told him I needed to discuss his marketing plans. He agreed and I left the office to meet with him. I had to get out of there. I found several things to discuss with Mr. Wright so I didn't return to the office that day.

After that, the office environment was almost unbearable. I spoke to no one and spent as much time as possible with my clients. Every morning, on the way to work, I prayed that God would give me the strength to see through another day and the wisdom to treat my fellow workers with kindness. But I didn't have the strength to be kind.

The Fourth of July was one of our favorite holidays. We all loved fireworks and we all loved summer. Julie was home for her only summer visit, so I spent the whole four-day weekend with Geoff, Julie, and Adam. I thought Mom was doing okay. She had been very quiet lately, and I missed a couple of Sunday visits with our summer activities and my new effort to redeem myself to Geoff.

Sunday night, Julie had gone back to Chicago, Adam was out playing basketball with friends, and Geoff and I were relaxing at home watching a movie when Maria called.

"Carrie, we're in the emergency room," she said. "Mom is having some trouble. I think you should come."

I dropped everything and took off for the hospital. I told Geoff I could be there a long time, so it was better I go myself. If things were really bad, I could call for him.

When I got to the hospital, Mom was still in the emergency room. She was in a bed with Maria and John by her side. Just as I walked in, an orderly came into the room to take Mom for tests. I gave her a quick kiss as she left.

I didn't need to ask. My look said everything.

John spoke first. "I went to see Mom today Actually, she asked me to come. She wanted me to look at her leg. When I got there, she said I just needed to clean her leg off. There was blood in her sock and water was running down her leg. I called Maria and neither of us knew what was happening, but we knew it wasn't good, so here we are. Mom didn't want to come, but we insisted."

"What on earth could that be?" I asked.

"The doctor who first saw Mom said it is most likely blood clots, but they have to do tests." Maria told me.

"Blood clots? That sounds odd and serious."

"I know," Maria sighed.

Mom was gone for nearly an hour. Shortly after she returned, a nurse came and said they would be moving her up to a room soon. Since it was Sunday and a holiday weekend, the staff was somewhat limited.

An hour later, we followed Mom up to an empty room. We sat outside for thirty minutes while they finished cleaning the room. A little later the doctor came in and said that Mom has several blood clots in her legs. The big danger, of course, was that they could move up to her heart or lungs. They would start her immediately on blood thinners. In the best case, she would be in the hospital for a week while they determined the extent of the clots and adjusted the blood thinners.

When Mom was asleep, Maria, John, and I went to the waiting room to talk.

I spoke first. "I thought Mom was doing well."

"I guess we all did," John replied.

"Maybe we were all too busy to notice things weren't very good," Maria offered.

"I'm afraid, from this point, we won't be able to leave her alone, at least not for any length of time," John added.

"Do you think it might be time to talk about a nursing home?" I asked.

"We have to wait and see what the doctor says," Maria answered. "It's way too early to make any plans. First, we need to help her through this crisis, but yes, we may be headed there."

"You know how Mom feels about a nursing home," John said. "She won't ever go and I don't want to force her."

"Maybe we won't have a choice," I was thinking more practical.

I was beginning to wonder if there was any situation for which John would consider a nursing home. I was thinking of my career. I had worked so hard for my recent success at Ryan Advertising, and now things were so difficult. I knew my career could not sustain another extended absence. As soon as those thoughts flooded my mind, I was ashamed of myself. How could I be thinking of my career while my mom was so ill? But what was I to do?

After an extended silence, I was again the first to speak.

"I guess we need to talk about a schedule for staying with Mom. I hate to say this, but things at work are really difficult now."

"Things at your work are always difficult," John replied, probably more sharply than he intended, but I fully got his meaning.

"We all have work issues, and I'm sure we will all do our part," said Maria, ever the voice of calm. "Carrie has a boss to deal with, John. We don't."

"Yeah, but we have a business to save," he replied sulkily.

"John," Maria offered gently, "Why don't you stay tonight, as long as you think necessary. I'll come early in the morning. Carrie can spell me whenever she can tomorrow and stay for the evening. By then we may know what we're dealing with and work out a schedule. How does that sound?"

We all agreed. Maria and I said good night to Mom and left together.

As we walked toward our cars, she said, "You know John, Bill, and I are feeling a lot of pressure to get our business out of the red. He doesn't mean to be sharp with you, but it's maybe harder for him than any of us. He and Mom have always been so close."

"I know, but I've been skating on thin ice at work for some time. I don't know how long Mr. Ryan is going to put up with this."

"Surely, he can't complain about missing work when your mother is in the hospital?" Maria asked.

I don't think Maria has ever had to deal with a person like Matt Ryan. She always sees the best in everybody, but not everybody has a best side.

"Sure, he can," I answered. "He couldn't care less what my situation is. And, the truth is, neither do our clients. When work has to be done, it has to be done. Deadlines have to be met. People may say they care, but they only care as long as it doesn't interfere with their projects. I almost understand where he's coming from. I just wish he didn't have to be so nasty about it."

"Being nasty never helps any situation," Maria said. "I just don't understand why people have to be nasty. What on earth do they accomplish like that?"

It was a rhetorical question that didn't require answering. We both knew that, so we finished our walk in silence.

I had to smile at Maria as she climbed into her truck. If only I could be more like her. She can't imagine people being nasty. I can hardly imagine anyone in business not being rude or unpleasant. If only I could live in her world.

Chapter 11
Fearing the Worst

I dreaded telling Mr. Ryan about my mother's new illness. It had to be done, so I would go in early and get it done as soon as possible.

I was already in the office when Mr. Ryan arrived. As soon as he had settled in with the first of his five cups of coffee, I knocked on the door.

"Can I have a minute of your time?" I asked.

"I guess this is important?" he questioned back, looking up from a huge stack of papers in front of him.

"Yes," I answered

"Come on in, if you must," he smiled. "What is it? Mom sick again?"

The shocked look on my face and lack of response said everything.

"Well, how much time do you think you should get off this time?" he said matter-of-factly.

"I don't really know," I said honestly. "Mom was admitted to the hospital last night, and we don't really know yet what is going on. I'd like to leave about three o'clock today, if that's okay. I'll probably need to work a reduced schedule this week, but I can keep my cell with me and take my laptop to the hospital to work on copy, if necessary."

"Whatever," he said, returning to his stack of papers. "Keep Jamie informed of your whereabouts. Make sure you tell her what to say to clients."

I had turned to leave the office, then stopped and turned back to Mr. Ryan. I had to rip off the other Band-Aid.

"I'm not sure that will work. For some reason, Jamie doesn't follow my direction. She just might tell clients anything."

Mr. Ryan looked up from his paper pile and pushed his chair back a bit.

"So, you're having trouble with Jamie."

"Well, yes. She gives clients wrong information, and she is anything but helpful to me."

"She is your subordinate," Mr. Ryan said. "If you don't like what she's doing, you should fire her."

"I didn't think I had that authority," I replied, startled.

"Well, you do. She works for you. If you can't get her to do what you tell her, you should fire her."

He was looking me square in the eyes when he said this.

"But she works for you too," I said, trying to figure out what he was thinking.

"Office assistants are a dime a dozen," he replied. "You need to step up and take control of the situation if you ever expect to get more responsibility," he said.

"All right, I'll think about it."

"Just make sure you can document an appropriate reason for firing," Mr. Ryan said, turning back to his paper pile.

I decided to do what Mr. Ryan said and carefully document our interaction. I sent her an email with explicit instructions for taking my calls while my mother was ill. I told her to put all her correspondence to me in writing and email me with any urgent client request while I was out. If I find clear violations of the instructions I gave her, and I could document them, then I'd fire her. It felt, for the first time in a long time, that Mr. Ryan was on my side.

I telephoned all my current clients and told them my mother was in the hospital and I may be harder to reach for a while. They all seemed sympathetic and understanding, but also a bit worried about their projects. Next, I had to face one of the more difficult tasks. I had to meet with Sam and go over everything I was working on.

Our meeting was cold, but professional. He was also sympathetic about Mom, but not friendly. Before we wrapped up our meeting, I decided to rip off another Band-Aid.

"Sam," I started, "I'm really sorry about what happened. I must have given you wrong signals. I've been married a long time and just don't know how to be friends without giving off the incorrect signals."

"It's okay," he said roughly. "I probably overreacted. I'm glad you said something. I don't want things to be so strange with us," he said kindly. "If you ever decide to change those signals, you'll let me know, won't you?"

"I won't change my signals," I replied emphatically.

He shrugged and walked off.

Surely, I thought, there must be some way to get along with men like Sam without sleeping with them. But I was lost for the answer.

I got to the hospital by 3:30 p.m. Maria had been there since seven a.m. and was glad to see me. Mom was sleeping when I arrived so we went to the waiting room to talk.

"How is she?" I asked.

"She feels pretty good. She's weak, but in good spirits. She doesn't quite understand why she has to be in here. She keeps saying we shouldn't have rushed off to the hospital. But the doctor says if we hadn't she wouldn't be alive today. He feels the clots surely would have traveled up to her heart and that would be all."

Maria's voice trailed off with a sob. I reached over and touched her hand.

"I know she's old and we should be prepared," she continued, "but I'm not."

"What does the doctor say about her prognosis?" I asked.

"He says it all depends on how well the blood thinners work for her. He thinks there are dozens of little clots throughout her leg, maybe other places. They just don't know yet. They'll have to monitor her carefully for a few days and see what develops."

"Is there anything else they can do?" I asked.

"He said they could put something in her thigh, like a screen that would prevent clots from traveling up," she said. "Doesn't that sound awful?"

"It all sounds pretty unbelievable.. Have you called church to ask for prayers?"

"Yes," Maria answered with another sniffle. "Pastor Mueller came and talked to her today. We all prayed together. It was lovely." She smiled. "I've been on the phone all day. I called my kids, our aunts and uncles, Mom's friends, everybody I could think of. It's exhausting calling all these people, but everybody wants to know."

"Why don't you go home and get some rest," I suggested. "I'll take over from here."

"Thanks. Just stay as long as you think necessary. John was awfully worn out this morning. He had to work today, too, so I don't think he'll be able to come back for a while. He's a guy you know; this is hard," she added. "Oh, I almost forgot. Can you come tomorrow morning? I have a doctor's appointment. It's taken me months to get this appointment, and I just don't want to miss it,"

"Okay," What else could I say?

We said goodbye with a hug and I walked back to Mom's room. She was just waking up. She turned and looked at me puzzled.

"I thought Maria was here," she said weakly.

"She was, but she had to go. I'll stay with you awhile," I added.

"But where's John?" she asked. "Isn't John coming?"

"No," I answered, a little testy. "John was here last night; Maria was here during the day; but now you've got me."

"I sure thought John and Maria would be here," she continued. "I don't understand why I need to be in the hospital. John just got excited and now I'm stuck here. I want to go home. Tell John I want to go home. He'll take me."

"Well, John and Maria will be back tomorrow and we can talk about it then," I lied.

It never stopped hurting that she preferred them, but I couldn't change that.

"The last time we talked," I started, "you told me about your wedding and how Grandma and Grandpa refused to accept it. With no place to live, where did you go?" I asked.

Actually, this question had been on my mind since she told me about her wedding. Now that she had opened the flood gates, I wanted to know everything.

"Well, your dad did some work for a very wealthy man named 'Niederhoff.' He had a large estate outside Kirkwood. Dad was a gardener for Mr. Niederhoff and knew that there was an empty outbuilding on the property with a damaged roof. Your dad and I went to Mr. Niederhoff and told him we had just gotten married and had no place to live. Joseph offered to repair the roof and fix up the shack if he allowed us to live there. I guess Mr. Niederhoff had a soft heart because he said yes. He said he'd even supply the building materials we would need.

"Your dad worked night and day on that shack. It had no running water or anything else that would indicate it was a place to live except four walls—and when your dad was done, a roof. But we made it home. I made curtains from old feed sacks and hauled water from a nearby spring and we thought we were in heaven. Of all the places I've lived in my life, I have to say that was my favorite. Maybe because it was so small our love couldn't get lost there, or maybe because we were blissfully happy," she smiled.

"How long did you live there?" I asked.

"It was only a little over a year that we lived there together. Then the war came. I thought my heart would break in two when your dad was drafted into the Army. He didn't really want to go, but he didn't have much choice. He got his notice and he left.

"I stood there at the train station as his train moved out on his way to Fort Leonard Wood, thinking I would never see him again. I thought my life was over. I couldn't go back to my parents' after the way they had treated Joseph, and I couldn't go back to our lovely little shack where we had so many great memories, so I went to the Augustines'. They took me on as a full-time cook. I lived there until Joseph returned, but it wasn't long. In a month he was home. The Army decided he had flat feet. I don't think there is any way I can describe how I felt when he walked in the backdoor at the Augustines'."

A tear was now trickling down her cheek. She didn't need any more words.

We were interrupted by a young nurse who came to take Mom's blood. They were taking blood quite often now to help determine the level of blood thinner required. The nurse was obviously a student.

"My mother is a hard stick," I told her. I was in no mood to let a student use my mother for a pin cushion.

"I'm pretty good," said the nurse and prepped Mom for taking blood.

As she pushed the needle in, I could see Mom grimace, although she'd never complain. The nurse grimaced as well, knowing she wasn't finding the vein.

"You're done here," I told her quickly. "Sorry, I don't mean to be rude, but Mom has enough pain. She doesn't need this. Can you get an IV technician?"

"Okay," the young girl said sheepishly. "I'll call someone else."

Shortly after the nurse left, Mom said she needed to use the bathroom. She had nearly lost the ability to stand, but was determined to get up and use the toilet. I rang for the nurse. Fifteen minutes later, I rang again. Another fifteen minutes, one more ring. Mom was getting desperate. She had a portable commode by her bed, but I wasn't sure I could manage her. I decided to find someone who could help. I found a likely candidate, a young orderly who looked strong and capable.

"My mother needs to go to the toilet and I can't get her up myself. Could you please help me?"

"You should ring for her nurse," the orderly said.

"I did ring, and ring and ring. No one's coming. She can't hold it any longer. Would you please help me?" I begged.

He gave me an understanding look. "Okay. We're supposed to have two people for a lift, but I'll never find another person today. I'll try."

It was awkward and uncomfortable for Mom, but we managed. Her feet kept slipping when we tried to get her to stand. If we pulled on her, it hurt. There didn't seem to be any easy way to do this. But she was much relieved when she finished. I thanked the orderly profusely. The IV nurse finally came in just as we were putting Mom back in bed.

"You can hurt her like that," she chided us. "You should have two aids and a lift belt," she added.

"And just where do you think we can get two aids?" I asked, my temper rising.

"Today is tough," she admitted. "We're a little short on staff and have a number of fall-risk patients like your mom. The best solution is to put a diaper on her and let her relieve herself in the diaper."

I'm not sure which shocked me more, the fact that they would encourage Mom to wet her pants or the fact that the nurse would admit that they were understaffed.

"I'm not wearing a diaper," Mom insisted. "I can get up and go to the toilet. I just need a little help. I'm not an invalid."

"Surely, you must realize how humiliating it is to suggest she wet herself," I snapped. "She's a grown, dignified lady who fully understands what's going on."

"I gave you the best answer I can," the nurse replied. "This is reality. Mrs. Schmidt is weak and unable to stand. We don't have sufficient staff to get her out of bed on demand. In these cases, a diaper is the best solution."

"Well, it's not the best solution for us. It may well come to that someday, just not today. We'll do the best we can."

Mom's dinner came and she ate with a healthy appetite. However, a little while after she ate, she started complaining of stomach pain. I ignored it for a while, but soon decided Mom needed some help. I called a nurse and told her mom needed something for pain. The nurse said she'd call the doctor and see what she could take. About a half an hour later, the nurse re-entered with some stronger pain meds.

I followed the nurse to the hallway and asked, "When will Mom see the doctor next?"

"Sometime tomorrow, I suspect," the nurse answered.

"I'd like to talk to him about her pain. It's different and more severe than any pain I've seen."

"Elderly people often complain of unspecific pain," she said. "It could be nothing."

"You don't know my mother. She's nearly had a finger chopped off and not complained. She had a heart attack and didn't tell anyone. I know this *is* something," I insisted.

"Well, you know her best," the nurse replied. "I will make a notation about the pain in the chart to make sure the doctor checks it out."

"I'd like to be here when the doctor comes," I told her.

"Well, then you should be here at six a.m.," she said and walked off.

It didn't take long for Mom to fall fast asleep. I left the hospital at eight p.m. and picked up a quick McDonald's hamburger on the way home. I was in bed by ten o'clock, but it took awhile to fall asleep. So many things kept racing through my mind. What would happen at work with new absences? What was this new pain? Would Mom ever be able to come home again? How would we pay for full-time nursing care or a nursing home? How would we ever convince Mom that either was needed?

Suddenly, I was floating over a little shack with a big hole in the roof. My parents were inside. They were both around forty, the age I remember from my childhood. They were eating dinner and laughing. Then I was falling, and we were in the house where I grew up. Dad was there, but I was puzzled because he was supposed to be dead. Mom was there, too, but she was very old and I didn't know how she got old. There was a big storm coming, and I was looking for Maria and John. The winds were whistling and making a ringing sound.

"Carrie, your alarm is going off," Geoff said. "Are you getting up?"

I was struggling to return to reality. It took a couple of minutes for me to figure out where I was and who I was.

"Carrie! Carrie!" Geoff shouted. That did the trick. Now I knew who and where I was. I was Geoff's wife, and he was pissed that the alarm was ringing at five a.m.

I jumped out of bed, but I was moving slowly. I quickly packed my bag with snacks and tea and ran off to the hospital. I arrived at 6:30 and the doctor was already in the room. He was asking Mom questions about the pain.

"So, when did you first feel this pain, Mrs. Schmidt?" he asked.

"Well, I've had pain like this on and off for many years," Mom replied, "but it was never quite this strong. It hurts really bad."

"On a scale of one to ten—" The doctor started with the standard question.

"It was around a fifty," Mom interrupted him.

The doctor smiled. "Well, we'll have to investigate a fifty. I'll order some tests today. Meanwhile, we're still concerned about the clots. We haven't got your blood at the right level just yet," he added.

"So, I can go home maybe tomorrow?" Mom asked, hopeful.

"I don't think tomorrow," the doctor replied, "but maybe by the end of the week."

"My bed at home is much softer," Mom told the doctor. "I think I'd rest better there."

He smiled and patted her hand.

I followed him into the hall.

"What do you think the pain is?" I asked.

"Well, at first I thought it could be her heart," he said, "but I'm not so sure. It could be her gall bladder, too, especially if she's had this pain for years. Has she ever had her gallbladder tested?" he asked.

"I know she had problems with it years ago, but she doesn't talk about pain much. If it is the gallbladder, can't you simply take it out?" I asked.

"For someone your mom's age and on blood thinners, nothing is simple," he replied.

I understood.

"We'll do some tests and watch her for the next few days," he continued. "But eventually we may have to make a decision on surgery. I'm not sure she can survive surgery. Both her age and the complications caused by the blood clots makes surgery risky. But if her gallbladder is causing pain, it's only going to get worse. Are you the person who would make this decision?"

"I have a brother and a sister. We should make the decision together."

"You should talk it over with them. I'd like your decision tomorrow. In any case, I don't think your mom will be able to return to her home. I would suggest a rehab facility for a few months, maybe longer."

I don't know why this was news to me, but it was, and I wasn't prepared.

"What do we do?" I asked, stunned.

"The hospital has a sister rehabilitation facility that we recommend in these instances," he said. "I'll have the nurse give you some literature."

With that he was off, and we were faced with a whole new challenge.

I quickly called Maria and told her what the doctor had said. She and John discussed the surgery. John was in favor of surgery and Maria was firmly against surgery. That left the deciding vote to me. Before I returned to Mom's room, I stepped into the chapel. I sat for a few minutes to have a little talk with God. I asked Him to help me figure out how to make this decision. I knew God would give me the answer, but I wasn't so sure I would be aware enough to catch it.

When I returned to Mom's room, she had just finished breakfast. She had more pain. In all my years, I had never seen Mom complain and grimace with pain. I was wondering if this was God's sign. We got more meds, but she needed a distraction, this time for a different reason.

"Mom, you told me yesterday about Dad returning after being released by the Army. What did you do next?" I asked.

"For a while, we were blissfully happy, again. It was like there was no war. We lived in Mr. Niederhoff's shack, but I stayed on as cook for the Augustines. At that time, all my friends, including my sister, Martha, and cousins, Laura and Emma, worked in rich houses. Laura was a cook for the Brinkmans. They were one of the richest families in St. Louis, and they were out of town a lot.

"Sometimes we would throw dinner parties for our husbands and boyfriends in their fancy dining room while they were gone. We used their elegant china and wine glasses. Laura was a master cook, and she would make some of the fancy dishes she made for the family. We'd all help. Your dad was such a clown. He'd come to the party with a tall top hat and tuxedo that he had found in a dump. He hated the little demitasse cups, so he'd pull out a giant coffee mug. He made us all laugh so much."

"Did you live like that throughout the war?" I asked.

"No, we grew more and more afraid that the government would change their minds about not needing your dad, and we decided to make a move that would keep him home for good," she said.

"What could keep him home?" I asked, eager.

"Well, you could be exempt from military service if you were involved in an *essential industry*," she said. "Farming just happened to be an essential industry. So, we got a job as caretakers on a chicken farm. We both knew plenty about chickens, growing up on farms with tons of chickens. We were hard workers, so we thought it would be easy. The job came with a lovely farmhouse to stay in. It was the prettiest little farmhouse I ever saw. Our boss, Mr. Reynolds, owned several farms, but he couldn't or didn't want to do the work. Most of our chickens were sold to restaurants. We'd kill and clean the chickens by hand and deliver them to the restaurants. They would pay Mr. Reynolds, and he'd send us a monthly check with a commission. The more chickens we'd raised and harvested, the more money we'd earn."

"That sounds like very hard work,"

"It was, but we were raking in the money and we had a lovely home to live in. Some days I think I harvested a hundred chickens. I'm sure I didn't, but it felt like that." Mom smiled.

"You must have lived in relative luxury."

"If happiness and hard work mean luxury, I guess so. But we hardly ever spent a dime of the money we earned. We ate eggs and chicken and anything I could grow on the little farm, which was substantial. We never bought anything new, and used little."

"But why?" I asked. "You had money."

"We also had a dream. We wanted a place of our own, a farm that we actually owned. We wanted to sell what we grew and keep the money, without a landlord taking most of it. We wanted the security of knowing that no one could change their mind and throw us out. I guess we wanted the American dream."

"Couldn't you just get a loan?" I asked.

"A loan?" she laughed. "First, you forget we had just had a depression. Loans were scarce, especially to two young people with no collateral. You actually had to have something to get a loan in those days. Nope, we knew the only way we would ever get a farm of our own was to save our pennies and pay cash, and we did."

"How long did it take you?" I asked.

"It took seven years," Mom answered, "seven long, happy years of hard work and saving."

"Wasn't Maria born during that time?" I asked.

"Yes," she smiled. "Three years before we moved to the farm you grew up on, we had Maria. When we finally had enough money for our farm, we started looking. The place we bought didn't have much. No house, no barn, just good farmlands, and the start of an orchard. We decided we wanted to grow fruit trees and that would take time. We found land that was good for growing trees. We had just enough to build a shed and start planting crops. We thought we could live in the shed for a couple of years and then build a house.

"Even though we had some success with the farm, the couple of years turned into ten years. You were born while we lived in the shed; John too. It wasn't a very easy place to have a baby."

The shed that I had called home my first ten years was three rooms: a bedroom where Mom and Dad and baby John slept, a living room with a roll-out sofa bed where Maria and I slept when I was old enough, and a small kitchen. The only source of heat was an oil-burning stove in the living room. We had running water, but no hot water. The bathtub hung on the wall of the garage. It took a lot of boiling water to take a bath. The toilet was outdoors, but we had a small ceramic pot in the kitchen corner. I couldn't help thinking, how on earth did Mom manage to recover from delivering a baby with no bathroom.

"It wasn't so bad, you know," she said. "What we lacked in convenience and luxury, we made up for in love. We had lots of good times in that little place. I'd watch TV and see all these stars that are in so much trouble, and I'd think how much better their lives would be if they traded in their mansions for a little three-room house filled with love.

"God was with us, you know. You see that more on a farm than in any other occupation. The farm grew miraculously. The orchards flourished and bore fruit in abundance. We bought more land and planted more orchards. We found out we could make money selling pumpkins—and vegetables too. We just kept adding. Then we built a comfortable house," she smiled.

"With not one, but two bathrooms," I added eagerly, memories flooding back. This part of the story I could remember. "How I loved having a real bathtub and a shower. Almost as much as I loved having our own room and twin beds," I laughed.

"It was—it is a beautiful house," she said. "It was our dream house. It might not be everybody's dream house, but it was ours. Only, it wasn't happy very long," she added sadly.

We only lived in our lovely new house six years before my father died of cancer. It wasn't long after we moved in, in fact, that he was diagnosed.

The next chapter of Mom's story was not one I was eager to relive. I knew it all too well.

Just then an orderly came to take Mom for testing. I wasn't paying much attention to which test they were doing. It all seemed to melt together. I only wanted to know to tell Maria, because she would surely ask.

I asked the orderly if I could go along.

He said, "The family usually just stays in the room or goes to the waiting room."

"I know, "but I want to come along."

"You can come as far as the Imaging Center waiting room," he answered. "If you want."

"I want," I smiled.

As we wheeled through the hospital, I could see Mom was in pain. "Is there anything I can do?" I asked her.

"I wish this cart wouldn't hit any bumps," she moaned.

"Please drive carefully. It's precious cargo," I told the orderly. Fortunately, he was a good-humored orderly and smiled.

The orderly stopped outside the Imaging Center and went in. I chatted with Mom as she lay on the gurney, nearly exposed, as tons of outpatients walked past. We tried to joke, but it wasn't very funny. I was glad I had come with them. It was hard enough for Mom to understand what was going on, without lying, endlessly, in a strange hospital corridor with nothing to do. It would be so much worse if she was alone.

After nearly a half hour, the orderly returned. "It's our turn now," he said.

I had lots of retorts ready to throw at him, but I knew it would do no good. The system wasn't his fault.

As I took my seat in the waiting room, I glanced at my watch. It was nearly noon. I couldn't believe so much time had passed. I had made no contact with the office all morning.

Before I called them, I checked on Maria.

"How has your morning gone?" I asked Maria when she answered my call.

I was hoping everything was well with her and she would hurry to the hospital so I could leave for work. But my luck wasn't that good.

"The doctor says I need a hip replacement." Maria said slowly. "I don't know what I'll do."

"I suppose you'll get your hip replacement?" I asked.

I could only think how much more work this would mean for me. I could barely handle my *mom* responsibilities as it was. If Maria was recuperating from surgery, my job would double. Of course, this was selfish, yet there it was.

"I can't possibly be out of commission for one or two months," she replied. "We'd have to put Mom in a nursing home. And who would replace me on the farm? It just can't be done."

"I'm very sorry," I managed to say, but I was actually thinking, thank goodness. WE can't handle this.

Quickly moving on to my problems, I added, "I really, really need to get to work. Can you come and sit with Mom?"

"Sure. I'll be there in about twenty minutes."

"We're in the Imaging Center waiting room."

"I'll find you," Maria offered.

When I hung up, I called the office. Jamie answered, "Hi, Jamie, do I have any calls?"

"Yes," she said. "Bobby Wright called. I told him you'd be in by noon. Sally called too. I just told her you weren't in because I didn't think you would be here by noon and I don't like lying."

"Why didn't you call me and let me know Bobby and Sally called?" I asked angrily. "Isn't that what my email said?"

"Your email said I should let you know if there were any problems," Jamie smirked back. "The only problem I saw was that you're not here. I told them what I was supposed to tell them."

"I think that's debatable. I'll be there in forty-five minutes. If anyone else calls, please let me know."

I was fuming now. I was mad enough to fire Jamie, but overwhelmed with the pressure of making such a life-changing decision for a young girl, no matter how much she irritated me. Just then Maria arrived. She was visibly shaken. I knew she wanted to talk, but I just wanted to get to the office.

"Oh, boy, Carrie, what am I going to do?" she asked. "I just can't afford to be out of commission."

Just then, the orderly wheeled Mom out. Saved, I thought. I can escape the serious discussion I knew Maria wanted to have and rush back to work. Mom looked tired and in pain.

"I'm so sorry," I lied. "I have to get to work. I'll come back after work." I rushed out.

On the way to the office, I called Bobby Wright and Sally. Bobby just had some minor details of the upcoming campaign he wanted to discuss. I made an appointment to meet with him the next day. Sally, on the other hand, was quite irate. It seems a marketing mailing that was supposed to be delivered today had not been mailed. This was going to be a much bigger problem. If only Jamie had talked with her, or called my cell, I could have been much more helpful.

When I got to the office, I had no time to confront Jamie. I had to race to my desk and start making phone calls to find out what happened to the mailing. It took all afternoon to unravel the mounting problems with the mailing gone awry. Sally was still pretty mad, but I was able to uncover a problem with their mailing house that had delayed the mailing. It was now in the mail and would be delivered on time, although not the optimal date. I promised to meet with Sally and her people tomorrow.

It was 6:30 when I left the office. I was determined not to have another McDonald's dinner, so I stopped at an upscale take-out deli and picked up a fresh-made chicken-salad sandwich. As I was leaving, I passed the bakery counter. It stopped me cold. There was a beautiful array of little pies and pastries. My first thought was how much Mom would love these little pies. I picked a lemon one to take her. I thought this would make our visit special.

When I got to the hospital, both Maria and John were there. I presented my little lemon pie to Mom to much delight. It made me feel so good to see her face light up. Maria said her evening meal was very disappointing and she had hardly eaten any of it. But the little lemon pie was gone in an instant. It was clear to me where my sweet tooth came from.

While Mom was finishing her pie, Maria, John, and I spoke in the hallway.

"The doctor said we have to give him an answer about the gallbladder surgery by tomorrow morning," she said. "He said all the tests were inconclusive. He thinks it is the gallbladder, but he can't prove it. This is such a difficult decision. I don't blame either of you for your vote, but I just can't vote for something that could end her life." Tears were flowing down her face.

"I understand," said John. "It's a momentously large decision. But I've seen her pain. I think we need to try the surgery."

Just then we heard a loud cry from Mom's room. We rushed in to see her writhing in pain. I quickly ran to get a nurse. She said the doctor happened to still be in the building and she'd call him immediately.

About fifteen minutes later the doctor arrived. He looked at us accusingly. "Has she had anything to eat, other than the prescribed hospital food?" he asked sternly.

I was shaking. Maria and John looked at me but nothing came out of my mouth. Maria understood my reluctance to speak.

"Yes," she said. "She had lemon pie."

"Lemon pie!" the doctor boomed. "Really?"

"Yes. I gave her a little lemon pie," my confession and tears pouring out.

"Well," said the doctor, "that was a very lucky thing. Lemon pie was the perfect test for the gallbladder. This immediate reaction tells me conclusively that her problem is most certainly the gallbladder. There is no more decision to be made. It will come out tomorrow as soon as I can put a proper surgical team together. My compliment to whoever thought of lemon pie."

"Well," said John, "you are to be congratulated, it seems. You went from villain to hero quicker than an ice cube melting in hell," he laughed.

With tears rolling down my face, I said, "The pie didn't come from me; it came from God. This morning I prayed that God would help me make this terrible decision. He did. He gave us lemon pie."

We laughed and hugged. Mom didn't quite understand, but we tried to explain it to her. We told her she would have her gallbladder removed tomorrow.

She said, "I've been wanting my gallbladder removed for years. If I knew all it would take was lemon pie, I would have tried that years ago."

We had a lovely evening, sharing and reminiscing. It was not at all like an evening before a life-threatening surgery. As I sat watching Maria, John, and Mom sharing memories, I closed my eyes and gave thanks to God for a little lemon pie.

Chapter 12

Lemon Pie Storm

Gallbladder surgery is pretty routine, but not this one. We all knew the risks. A big surgery requires big plans. Before we left the hospital, we had called Pastor Mueller and asked him to come and pray with Mom before surgery. Maria and I had each called our kids and filled them in. We called Mom's siblings too. We knew they were concerned. Then we each contacted our friends to ask them to pray.

I was so exhausted when I fell into bed, nothing could keep me from sleep. But I woke up suddenly at 4:30 a.m. and remembered, I had major appointments today. With all the events of the previous day, work had faded into distant memory. Now I was in trouble. There was nothing I could do at 4:30 a.m., but worry.

I was dressed and ready to head out the door at six o'clock. I stopped by the office before going to the hospital to pick up my laptop and some papers. It was going to be a long day at the hospital and I could spend some of the time working, I thought.

On the way to the hospital, I called Maria.

"I'm so sorry to call so early, but I just realized that I have some critical appointments today. I don't know what I can do about it."

"Yeah, Bill says I have to be here to handle some critical office work," Maria said. "If I don't get these bills paid, we could literally lose services to the store. I was so hoping you and John could cover for me today. I can be there all day tomorrow."

My appointments weren't tomorrow. They were today. I couldn't leave Mom alone before the surgery. I thought I could at least sneak out for the appointment with Sally at Goodman's.

I walked into Mom's room at seven a.m. She was awake. A nurse was there taking blood. As usual, she couldn't find a vein. I requested an IV technician and she went to find one.

Just as the IV technician finished, the doctor entered. He said the surgery was set for one o'clock. Mom's cardiologist was going to do some tests before the surgery, and he would stay for the procedure to monitor Mom's heart. They would come and get her at twelve noon.

It seemed we were suddenly engulfed in a flurry of activity. One nurse had papers to sign. Another had a portable heart monitor to check Mom's heart. Another was asking questions to determine her mental status. As soon as the flurry died down, Pastor Mueller came in. Mom was so glad to see him. We had a nice chat and he read from Psalms and offered a lovely prayer that made me cry. When he left, Mom was exhausted and tried to sleep. I sat in a chair and looked at my watch. Ten o'clock!! How did it get so late? The last time I had checked it was eight. I completely missed the meeting with Sally at Goodman's. I ran from the room and called Sally. She wasn't in. I left a message. I called the office. Jamie answered.

"Where did you disappear to? We thought maybe a bus hit you on the way to work," she smirked. "You wouldn't believe the uproar around here. I think you're in big trouble."

I could just imagine her smile.

"My mother is having surgery today," I started to explain, but I really didn't want to get into this with Jamie. "I need to talk with Mr. Ryan."

"Well, Matt's at lunch," she offered. "Lunch with Sally at Goodman's. He's trying to save your ass, I think. Too bad he had to run off to cover for you."

"Just tell him I'm stuck in the hospital and I'll be in tomorrow," I told her, holding my temper to a simmer.

"Not sure you need to come in tomorrow, but I'll tell him anyway."

I called his cell and left a message. I wasn't too sure it would matter, but I tried. Next, I called Bobby Wright. He was sympathetic and said we could meet tomorrow. I was grateful.

By the time I finished my calls, John was there. There was more activity with nurses and papers. One nurse asked John and me if we wanted to hire a night nurse. She explained that Mom would be brought back to this floor in the post-op section, but it wasn't full-time care. She said many families of patients in Mom's condition, not critical enough for ICU, but not well enough to speak for themselves, hire night nurses. She left us with a list of private services.

This required Maria's input, so John and I called her. She agreed to hiring a night nurse for at least the first two nights. When I hung up, I noticed the orderlies coming to take Mom to surgery. John and I kissed her and wished her the best. She smiled bravely and said to order more lemon pie. When she was gone, we hugged and cried.

The nurse told us we had to leave the room and suggested a waiting room. Mom wouldn't be coming back to this room in any case, she said. It seemed like a little sanctuary. I was sorry to leave it. The nurse promised to come and get us when her new room on the post-surgery wing was ready. We moved our substantial stuff to the waiting room and began the long vigil.

John and I were both deep into our laptops, managing missed business. I sent apology emails to everyone: Mr. Ryan, Sally, and Mr. Wright. I also sent emails to my creative team so they would hear from me, not Jamie, what had happened. I hoped this would ease the difficult return tomorrow. Then I got busy researching night nurses and calling agencies. Finally, I found two alternatives, discussed them with John, and got approval from Maria. I called and arranged a nurse for the next two nights. We hoped Mom would be well enough to manage the hospital nurses after that.

The long wait was beginning to wear on us. Mom had been gone almost three hours with no word. While John started pacing, I called Geoff and told him not to expect me for dinner. I don't think Geoff ever expected me for dinner these days, if he expected dinner at all. I talked to Adam and wished him well as he was off to basketball camp at the University of Missouri.

This was a very big deal for Adam to go to this camp. It didn't mean he would or could get a basketball scholarship, but it couldn't hurt either. In any case, it should improve his game and he was very excited about it. I wanted to be there to help him pack and give him a hug.

I reviewed the whole list of things he should take and he replied, "Got it, Mom," to each one. I'm glad he didn't see the tears running down my face as I told him I loved him and wished him great success at camp.

John looked up. He had been listening.

"I'm sure Adam will do well at camp," he said, trying his best to be supportive. John was Adam's godfather, but didn't spend a lot of time with him. Since John was a bachelor, we didn't always have much in common. We lived in different worlds and traveled in very different circles. Even as kids, we were never all that close. But it didn't change the fact that we did love each other. It just made it harder to be close.

"I've been missing so much of their lives lately, I hardly know how to be a wife and mother anymore. I should be home to help Adam pack and make dinner for Geoff," I said sadly.

"They will understand," John replied. "After all, they care about Mom too."

"I don't think they really understand. Not really. Sure, they say they do. They try their best to be supportive. But I can't make up this time we've missed. The basketball games I've missed, the evening meals I didn't make, the evenings I just wasn't there."

"I think you've way overblown this," John said. "Years from now, when they all look back, they won't remember the days you were missing. They'll remember the times you were together. Didn't you have a great Fourth of July together?"

"I guess you're right," I said.

"I think you're a terrific mom," John said looking straight at me for the first time all day. "I guess we don't have much opportunity to talk, but I just want you to know, I've noticed how hard you work at everything, helping take care of Mom, taking care of your kids and Geoff, and I'm always in awe at what a fantastic business woman you are. Sometimes Maria and I just marvel at you. Seems you got an extra share of family brains and ability."

I had no answer. Tears were streaming down now. It would have been easier for me if he was totally distant and self-centered. Why did he have to be so understanding and loving? He has just melted away all our distance.

I got up and gave him the biggest bear hug I could muster. "You're a pretty spectacular brother too," I managed to say.

Just as I sat back down, a nurse came around the corner.

"Since it's been such a long time since your mom went to surgery, I wanted to give you an update," she said politely. I looked at my watch and it was four p.m. I was shocked. I had no idea that so much time had passed.

"Your mom came through the surgery very well," she said, "for her age and medical conditions. We're watching her carefully in post-op, so it will be some time before she can come up here."

"Can we see her now?" I asked.

"No, sorry," the nurse replied. "We can't let you into post-op, but we can give you updates."

As quickly as she came, she was gone. The news we were waiting for was here. The long wait was over. We hardly had time to worry.

John quickly called Maria and gave her the news. I called Geoff, Julie, and Adam. Then John and I divided up Mom's siblings and each called two. Now the waiting seemed unbearable. We desperately wanted to see Mom. All our day's work was done and we were more aware of waiting.

I suggested to John that we do some research on rehab facilities. He found a few on his computer and we read some information. The big question was how much would Medicare and Mom's insurance pay? We were hungry, but we didn't want to risk being gone when Mom came up. John found a vending machine and got us each some high-calorie, sugary snacks.

Before long, our friendly nurse was back. She told us Mom was awake and ready to move to a room, but there was no room for her. A room had been vacated, but wasn't yet cleaned. They would bring her up as soon as the room was cleaned. It was six p.m. now and we were getting restless. John found a movie on his computer, something light, and we watched, hungry and tired. It was nearly eight p.m. when they finally wheeled Mom up to the room. We were very glad to see her, but she looked terrible. Her face was drawn and her skin very white.

She opened her eyes and said, "Can I eat lemon pie now?" We laughed. "I guess I'll be all better now," she smiled.

She was actually thrilled that the gallbladder that had troubled her for so many years was finally gone. I think, in her mind, she thought with this surgery she would be completely well. The gallbladder was something she could understand. It was a specific aliment linked to a specific organ. But the blood clot problem and the congestive heart failure she simply couldn't wrap her mind around.

The sad part was we understood her health was rapidly declining. Even though she had come through surgery well, it would leave her very weak, unable to walk on her own and needing much more medication. We had already seen, as the medications increased, her mental health and other normal bodily functions decrease. For every medication that kept her alive, there were side effects that made that life more difficult. We had seen increased urinary tract infections, vaginal infections, loss of bladder control, constipation or, at times, diarrhea, loss of appetite, trouble sleeping, trouble staying awake, and increasing memory loss.

I watched her sleeping for a little while, relieved that she was doing well, but wondering what her future held. I had insisted that John go and find something to eat. He returned shortly with a McDonald's bag and large drink.

"I'm going to stay until the night nurse comes," he said. "Why don't you go home. Tomorrow is another big day."

On the way home, I had a little talk with God. I asked him to help me find a solution to my work problems. *"Please, God,"* I prayed. *"Help me find a way out of this darkness to a better light."* I had no clue what was in store for me, but I should have remembered: be careful what you ask for.

I struggled to get out of bed the next morning. This had been a brutal week. Thank goodness it was Friday. I felt like I had been running a marathon all week. I suppose in a way I had.

I didn't want to be late for work, but it was going to be hard to face them too. On my way to work, I again asked God to help me find a way out of the jam I was in at work. I didn't want to be around people that made me spiteful and sneaky. I wanted so much to be kind, but I just couldn't manage it. But I knew, with God's help, I could do better. I strolled in at 8:35 a.m., just a few minutes late. As I was unpacking my briefcase, Mr. Ryan came into my office.

"Carrie," he said, "I'd like to see you in the conference room."

"Okay. I'll be right down."

"I'll be waiting for you," he returned with almost no emotion.

It was odd that he wanted to meet me in the conference room; but I thought if he was going to give me a tongue lashing, this was less public than his office.

"Close the door," he said solemnly as I entered.

Boy, I thought, this is going to be harder than I imagined.

"Yesterday was pretty inexcusable," he started. "Because of your disappearing act, Goodman's is ready to fire us. I don't think Mr. Wright is going to stay either."

"You do know my mother had surgery yesterday?" I asked, at a loss for words.

"The trouble is," said Mr. Ryan, "I don't think you know how important our work is. It's not something you can do occasionally, when everything at home is running smooth. You have an important role here and we have to have someone who is willing to make the sacrifice to be here."

"I know yesterday was inexcusable," I offered. "I'm sorry. I wish I could promise that it won't ever happen again, but I can't. I can only promise to always do my best."

"I'm afraid your best just isn't good enough," said Mr. Ryan. "Did you fire Jamie like I suggested?"

"I wasn't able to document an incident that merited termination," I said becoming increasingly more concerned. I certainly didn't like where this was going. Suddenly, sitting in the hospital with a critically ill mother seemed like a picnic.

"But you said she was undermining you. You should have fired her. Carrie, you just don't have the toughness to do the hard tasks this job entails. I have to let you go."

"Oh, Just like that?"

Nothing else would come out of my mouth.

"Fired? After ten years, just like that?"

I knew I was repeating myself, but nothing else would come out. There were so many things I thought of saying. But they didn't come out. This was so unfair. It wasn't my fault that Mom was sick. It wasn't my fault that she needed surgery—oh, yeah, the lemon pie—maybe it was. Was this all God's plan to help me resolve my work situation?

Yes, I thought, I prayed for a solution, and God gave me a solution. God knows what you need even if you don't.

"Why on earth are you smiling," barked Mr. Ryan. For the first time in this most difficult interview, he was raising his voice.

"It's okay. I think it's all God's plan."

"God's plan that I should fire you? Your God has a pretty odd sense of humor. Aren't you going to fight back?"

"Yes, my God does have a sense of humor," I smiled. "And no, I'm not going to fight. Please tell me what I can take."

"Take anything you want," he said with a note of disappointment. "Well, not the client files. I'll have Jamie bring you a box."

"No thanks, I'll get a box from storage. I'll be fine."

"If you say so," he muttered. "Damn strange girl. I think she's losing it," I heard him mutter under his breath. Honestly, I think he was so prepared for a fight he didn't know how to handle my acceptance of the situation. He was baffled.

I wanted to laugh out loud, but I was afraid Mr. Ryan might have me committed. Maybe it was all the stress that had built up over the last few days. Maybe it was the tremendous relief that the troubles of this office were behind me, but I felt more like dancing than crying. I didn't have a clue what I would do next. I just knew it would not be in this place.

I packed as quickly as I could. It's amazing how many little trinkets from home you manage to amass in your office in ten years. I found little things my kids had made for me and trinkets vendors had gifted to me. I also found a list of my clients and contacts that I had made for Christmas cards last year. This was better than a Rolodex. At the very least it could help me find a new job. I stuffed it in my briefcase along with a few other helpful things. When I finished, I had a packed briefcase and a rather smallish box. I stood and looked at it for a minute. I wondered how ten years of work could boil down to this: one small box and briefcase. It just didn't seem like much.

As I looked up, I saw Sam approaching. He had a very sad, worried look on his face. The thought crossed my mind; I bet he thinks this is about him.

"Carrie, I'm so sorry," he said and tried to reach out for a big hug. "I hope I didn't have anything to do with this. What will you do?"

Poor Sam. He really does think this is about him. I did my best to shorten the hug.

"I'll be fine. I'm sure I'll find something."

I took a deep breath and looked up. The rest of the art department was staring at me. I did have some good times here I thought. I do enjoy the work. I wonder if I'll ever enjoy working again.

"I will miss this place," For the first time, I was feeling sad and fighting back tears.

"I'll miss you," Sam said a little teary-eyed.

I patted him on the shoulder. "This was just meant to be," I added somewhat philosophically. "Life goes on."

Sam didn't know how to respond. I'm not sure what they all expected me to do, but I was obviously disappointing them. I picked up my things and walked out. I had to stop by Mr. Ryan's desk for my severance check and the COBRA information. I entered Mr. Ryan's office for the last time. He handed me a check and a pamphlet on COBRA. I didn't look at the check. It was what it was. I was leaving and didn't want to argue or delay. I had my future to think about, and Mom. I had nothing more to say to him.

"I'm going to record this as a workforce reduction so you can apply for unemployment if you want," he said.

"Thanks," I replied. "I will do that. I don't think I'll need the COBRA. I can get insurance from Geoff's office."

"Good," he said. "That helps me. I do wish you all the best."

"I wish you much success too," I said and I meant it. "Goodbye."

As I turned the corner, I saw Jamie. I didn't know what to say to her. I suppose this wasn't her fault. Maybe she just didn't like me, and there was never anything that would change that. Maybe she just needed a little love. After all Jesus said, "Love your enemies."

I took a deep breath and walked up to Jamie. I put my box and briefcase down. She took a step back, but I went up to her and gave her a big hug. She was a bit stunned. I'm sure she hadn't figured on this.

"I'll miss you," I lied. "I wish you all the best"—that was the truth. "I hope everything turns out just like you want it to." Actually, I knew it already had. She did too.

"Yeah, so long," she replied, obviously confused. "Best to you too."

I knew she didn't quite mean that either, but it didn't matter now.

I turned and walked out, got in my car, and drove off. Suddenly the finality of it all hit me. I've just turned my back on ten years of driving to this office, working with these people, eating lunch here every day, sometimes with friends. For all of its faults and difficulties, this job had become my identity. In an instant I had lost all that.

I pulled my car into a filling station and started to weep. I'm not even sure what I was crying for, but tears were flowing fast and furious. When I finally took a breath and looked up, I saw the hustle and bustle of a busy morning at the Quick Mart. Life went on just as it did when I was at work, when I had a job, and my mother was healthy. Suddenly, I realized life would go on for me too.

As quickly as the tear flood began, it was over. I never shed another tear over Ryan Advertising. I pulled out of that Quick Mart ready to embrace the next chapter.

Chapter 13

A New Chapter

By the time I pulled into my garage, I was fully ready to move on. As I opened the car door, I heard the phone ringing. I dashed into the house to answer it, thinking it was something about Mom. The voice on the other end startled me. It was Bobby Wright.

"Hello, is this Carrie Young?" he asked.

"Yes, it is," I answered. "Is this Bobby Wright?"

"Yes, it is," he answered. "What on earth is going on? I just got a call from Matt Ryan that you have left his agency for personal reasons."

It took a few seconds to collect my thoughts before I answered.

"Well, it seems more to me like I was fired," I answered as honestly as I could.

"This wasn't your decision?" he asked.

"No, it wasn't" was all I felt like saying. Actually, that's all I really knew.

"What are your plans?" he asked.

"Well, this is very recent," I replied. "I'm actually just getting over the shock. I haven't given a lot of thought to what I'm going to do."

"Why don't you start your own agency?" he said. "You'd make a great entrepreneur. I'm launching a new company and I want your marketing direction. I've never been a big fan of Matt Ryan's, you know. I'm only with him because of you and your ideas. I'd like to continue to work with you."

Now, I was really in shock. I never expected this. Before I fully had my thoughts gathered, I heard myself saying, "That's an excellent idea, Bobby. I believe I will do just that. It will take me a bit to pull things together, but can I count you as my first client?"

"Count me in," he said. "Call me when you're up and running. I'd sure like to see what you can do on your own."

Yes, I thought. I'd like to see that to. Could I really do this, I wondered.

As I hung up, a whole new prospect lay before me. I never considered starting my own firm. It's scary, but so is breathing. Maybe this was the kick I needed to jump into my own business. I wonder what would Geoff think. *Geoff!* I haven't told him I'm out of work.

Quickly, I gave Geoff a call. He was neither surprised or concerned. He had insurance covered, and he thought his salary would get us through just fine. He thought it was the best thing that could have happened because Ryan Advertising had overworked and overstressed me.

I had no idea Geoff felt like this. He managed the budget so tightly I figured he would panic at the loss of income. I did have a healthy severance. That helps. It would probably be enough to get the ball rolling on my own company.

Could I really do this? I was feeling more confident every moment.

The phone rang again. It was Sally Brinkman from Goodman's. She, too, had gotten a call from Matt Ryan that I had left for "personal reasons." She, too, encouraged me to start my own company and promised to give me a small piece of their business when I was up and running.

This was the biggest surprise of all. I would never have guessed she would land in my corner.

The phone rang again. It was Maria. "I was wondering if you were coming to the hospital today or do you have to stay at work?" she asked.

Oh, Mom, I forgot. With all that had happened today, the drama of the past few days and Mom's surgery had slipped my mind. That was another point on the plus side for losing my job.

"No, I don't have to stay at work. I got fired today."

"What!" Maria nearly screamed. "I'm so sorry Carrie. Was it because of Mom's care?"

"I'm not sure," I replied. "Maybe, partly, I don't know. I suppose it was the culmination of a lot of things. Missing yesterday was just the last straw."

"I'm so sorry," Maria said for the second time. "Is there anything I can do?"

"No, not really. It's all right. No, it's good. I'm actually glad it happened."

"Then me too. I hated the way they treated you there."

Did everyone see this but me? I wondered.

"That seems to be the most repeated phrase," I laughed. "Enough about me, how's Mom?"

"She's some better, but very weak," Maria said. "At least she's in good spirits," she said. "She thinks she can go home now, but that isn't going to happen. I hope she will be able to understand."

"I'll come up to the hospital now," I offered.

"You don't have to," Maria said. "I'm so sorry about your job."

That was three sorrys.

Shortly, I left for the hospital. Mom seemed like a good distraction today. I didn't want to think any more about Ryan Advertising and my next move. I just wanted to be with Mom.

On the way to the hospital, I called Julie and told her what had happened. She mirrored the sentiment I had already heard from Geoff and Maria. I felt I would probably hear that a few more times. It was not at all what I expected, but then I had never been fired before. I guess I was blind to how bad things were there. Hanging in is good, to a point, I suppose. In any case, it was very good to know that nearly everyone in my life was supportive and no one thought it signaled the end of my career.

Mom was still awfully groggy. We spoke only a little. She kept falling asleep. Maria said she had been doing that all day. John was taking the day off after staying late and working all day.

I told Maria to go; she had been there all day. After a couple more I'm so sorrys, she finally went. I stayed until the night nurse came, about nine p.m. I went over Maria's notes from the day with her, thanked her for her service, and took off.

When I walked in the door of my house, it had a different smell—the smell of lilies. There, on the kitchen table, was big bouquet of fresh lilies. Geoff was watching a movie in the living room. I went in and snuggled next to him.

"Thanks for the flowers."

"I thought you could use a little brightening today," he smiled and gave me a little kiss.

"It's perfect. Where's Adam?"

"On a date, I think," Geoff said. "He said he'd be home by eleven."

I looked at my watch. It was 9:30. "What can we do for an hour?" I asked with a sly smile.

"I don't know about an hour," Geoff smiled back, "but I do know something we can do."

The day that had started so horribly, ended beautifully. Before I drifted off to sleep, I said a little prayer thanking God for knowing what I needed, even when I couldn't see it.

The next day, I was at the hospital by seven a.m., as I had promised Maria. Since I didn't have a job to worry about, my time was my own.

There was much to do to put together a new business, but it could wait a couple of days. I wanted to enjoy my freedom, and Mom needed me here. The doctor came in at eight. He pronounced Mom improving quickly. He was amazed at her progress. Doctors always seemed to be amazed at her resilience. The doctor asked to speak with me in the hall.

"I think we will be ready to release your mom in a day or two," he said. "Have you decided on a rehab facility?"

"Well, my brother and I have discussed it, but we haven't made any decisions yet. Do you have a recommendation?"

He pulled a brochure from his file. Obviously, he's thought about this too. "This is the facility that is associated with our hospital. It's only two miles from here and easy for doctors to visit, or for us to come get her if her recovery doesn't go well. I'd be happy to see if they have a bed."

"I think I'd like to visit it before we make a decision," I replied.

"Sure. Just don't take too long. We can't keep her here much longer. She's in no immediate danger and we have no more treatment for her. Insurance may cover some of the rehab facility, but it won't allow us to keep her beyond the allocated time."

"Okay," was all I could think to say.

We knew this was coming, but with everything else that was going on, it had slipped my mind. It would, of course, be easy to just say okay to the doctor's suggestions, but this was my mother. We couldn't make this decision so lightly.

I called Maria and told her what the doctor had said. She said to make an appointment to visit the recommended facility and she would come. The Gate House was very accommodating and said we could come at ten a.m.

When I arrived, I was surprised to see a building that looked much like St. Mark's. It was a stark box building seven stories tall. Maria and I were conducted on a tour by a surly nurse that wanted to do anything but conduct a tour. She said the PR lady was off today. She only worked three days a week, unlike the nurses who were there all the time.

We apologized, but explained we didn't have time to wait. Our mother was being released in a couple of days. She added that all the patients from St. Mark's come there; she didn't quite understand why we wanted the tour.

When the tour was finished, Maria and I went to the coffee shop across the street to talk.

"Did you see what they were preparing for lunch?" Maria asked.

"Yeah. It looked like meat covered with yellow paint. Mom would never eat that."

"I know," Maria replied. "I thought rehab facilities were less like a hospital and more like apartments or retirement homes. That place is more like a prison than a retirement home. It was so, I don't know, institutional," she said with an air of defeat in her voice.

"I know what you're saying," I replied. "The halls were so stark and there was construction going on. Mom will hate this. I know the hospital recommends this place, but surely there must be something better. I just can't see Mom in there with no connection to the outside world for a month."

"Me neither," said Maria.

Just then I remembered that John and I had looked at a list of rehab facilities on my computer. Fortunately, it was in my car.

I pulled it out and we started looking online. We found one that was only three miles away. I called them and they said we could come right over. This time it wasn't the PR lady's day off and she met us cheerfully. This place was called the "Garden House" and it lived up to its name. You could hardly see any bare walls for all the plants, flowers and pictures of flowers. They had extensive gardens all around the one-story facility. It was sort of a wagon-wheel construction with the main large room for the cafeteria and recreation in the center and patients' halls spoked out from there. None of the halls were very long, or at least it seemed that way. It looked more like a college campus than a hospital, or prison.

We watched as they served a well-balanced lunch with fresh fruit and veggies. The cafeteria was bright and cheerful. They even had a bird cage in the main hall. You could hear the birds chirping everywhere.

"This is much more our mother's personality," Maria said. "Can we move her in as soon as she's released from St. Mark's?"

"Fortunately, we do have an opening," Mrs. Anderson told us. "We can send a van to pick her up from St. Mark's."

"Can the doctors from St. Mark's visit her here?" I asked.

"Yes, most of the St. Mark's doctors can visit here, but we have staff doctors too," she told us.

"How about therapy?" Maria asked.

"We visited our therapy rooms on the tour," said Mrs. Anderson. "She will most likely have therapy two or three times a day. This may be a place of rest, but a lot of work goes on here, too, to get her ready to return home. She'll have physical therapy, of course, but she'll also have occupational therapy to reteach her normal daily actives, like fixing meals."

"What about religious services?" I asked.

"We have a nondenominational service at ten o'clock on Sunday," said Mrs. Anderson. "It's led by a Presbyterian minister, mostly," she added.

"That will work," I said, smiling to Maria.

We both knew anything short of the traditional Lutheran was not Mom's choice, but we also knew it would work.

We signed the papers. Next, we had to contact the insurance company to make sure the Garden House was covered and fill out endless paperwork at the hospital. We felt good about our choice. We were very glad we had made the effort to visit the recommended facility and find a better alternative.

The day came for the transition. We weren't quite sure how much Mom understood about the move. She was certain that she could go home, even though she wasn't able to get to the bathroom herself. I believed, someplace in her addled mind, she believed she could walk to the bathroom. Our greatest fear was that she would try and fall. We all knew a major fall would be life-threatening.

I watched as the orderlies lifted Mom into a wheelchair and wheeled her out the door of the hospital. They loaded her in the van and strapped the wheelchair down with belts and buckles. She looked terrified. I smiled fighting back tears and said, "I'll see you at the Garden House."

All the way there I cried. It was just so hard to see this once vital, independent woman seated, strapped, and buckled like livestock.

We arrived at the Garden House, full of hope. Mom was still like the proverbial deer in headlights. I'm not at all sure she understood what was happening. I had volunteered to supervise the move because, well, I didn't have a job. Maria and John still had a business and needed to keep it running.

When we arrived, Mom was whisked to a two-person room. It seemed charming to me, but not to Mom. It was not at all what she was used to. I tried to distract her by pointing out the colorful artwork and the first-floor view of the gardens. She was appeased, but not amused. She had many questions that I couldn't answer to her satisfaction or understanding.

"What is this place?" she asked.

"It's a rehab facility," I answered.

"Why am I here?" she asked.

"The hospital couldn't keep you any longer, and you weren't well enough to go home," I answered.

"Why can't I go home?" she asked.

"The doctors want you to recover more before you go home. They will help you relearn to walk and regain use of your hands here," I said, trying to be thorough but forgetting her limited understanding.

"Is this a nursing home?" she asked. "Have you put me in a nursing home? Where's John? Where's Maria? They'll take me home."

"No, Mom, it's not a nursing home. John and Maria will be here shortly. We all want you to get well."

"How long will I have to be here? I want to go home," she moaned.

"We want you to go home too. I don't know how long you'll be here. When the doctor says you're healed, you can go home. It might be a month or two."

"A month or two!" she exclaimed. "Where's my phone? I need to call John."

In the midst of all these questions and Mom's increasing agitation, the nurse was pushing a stack of papers my way that had to be signed. An administrator came in and asked to see my power of attorney. I didn't have one, I explained, but my brother did.

"We'll have to have him come and sign some of these papers," the administrator told me.

"I'll call him," I answered.

I was growing increasingly worried about Mom's agitation. I knew this wasn't good for her on many levels. I told her I'd be back soon and headed down the hall to find a nurse and get some calming meds for Mom while trying to call John. I reached them both at the same time.

"You need to come and sign some papers," I told John on the phone while looking at the nurse.

"Why should I sign papers?" asked the nurse.

"No, not you," I said, still on the phone with John. "I want you to give my mother something to reduce her agitation."

"How can I give you meds for Mom?" asked John. "I don't think the rehab center would allow that."

"No, not you," I said to John and the nurse in front of me.

Then in an exasperated attempt to straighten things out, I told John on the phone, "Could you hold on just a second?"

I lowered the phone and repeated the request to the nurse. She roughly informed me that we would have to get a prescription from the doctor to get additional medication. So, I asked how I can find the doctor. She informed me that the doctor would see Mom tomorrow morning and she could ask him then. She turned and walked away. My heart sank. I had hoped for so much more from this lovely place.

I picked the phone up and told John he needed to come and sign papers. He was tied up with work, but would come as soon as he could. That was the best either of them could give me. With my heart heavy, I walked back into Mom's room. I noticed the nurse light was on.

"What do you need?" I asked.

"I have to go to the bathroom," she said. "I've had the light on since you left."

I walked down the hall again to the nurse's station. "My mother needs to go to the bathroom," I told the attendant at the station who was casually munching on lunch.

"Did you turn your call light on?" she asked.

"Yes, some time ago," I answered. "Mom can't wait very long,"

"Can she walk to the bathroom?" she asked, popping more food into her mouth.

"If she could, we wouldn't need help," I replied, a little testier than I intended.

"I'll call for a lifter," she smirked, ignoring my sarcasm.

I returned to Mom's room to find her more agitated.

"I need to go the bathroom," she repeated.

"Someone will come shortly. Let's unpack. Look, I brought you some things from home that Maria left with me yesterday. Here you can wear your own gown or pants and shirt. Where should I put these things?"

"I don't care. In the drawers there, I suppose," she said, pointing to the only set of drawers on her side of the room. "I don't like this place and I have to go to the bathroom.'

I started putting some things in drawers, when two orderlies came into the room pushing a huge machine with mechanical arms.

"What's this?" I asked.

"It's a lifter. Didn't you say you needed a lifter?"

"Well, I guess, but I didn't know what a lifter was," I replied.

"This is it," he said, pushing the monster next to Mom.

"Now, ma'am, all you need to do is raise your arms and we'll put this belt around you. And the sling under you. The lifter lifts you up and carries you to the toilet, where we lower you on the toilet."

"Can't you just help me walk?" asked Mom, truly terrified.

"This is the safest way to move you for us and you," he told her.

In horror, I watch my terrified mother being hoisted in the air by this monster machine and dropped to the toilet. Too late though. Whether from fear or just waiting too long, it all came out on the bathroom floor. Nonetheless, they set her on the toilet, where she deposited a little more before being hoisted back to her bed. The orderly quickly left to get supplies to clean the mess.

It took Mom a few minutes to recover. "I'll never do that again," she said firmly. "I'd rather die or wet myself than do that again."

"I don't blame you. I'll have a talk with the head nurse and tell her that thing is out. I'm sorry. I guess I can see why it would be helpful, but it's horrible. I'm so sorry."

I felt fully responsible for putting Mom through this torture. I helped pick this place; I agreed that a lifter was fine. What do I know? I have no experience to make any of these decisions.

When John and Maria arrived, Mom was finally sleeping.

"We need to have a talk with an administrator and head nurse," I told them. "Things have not gone well since we came here." Then I told them about the indifferent nurses, the difficulty in getting medications to calm Mom, and the monster lifter.

"Oh, my Lord," said Maria. "I thought this was going to be an easy phase. This place looks so nice."

"No place can be better than the staff," said John, "and that's very hard to evaluate."

I was relieved that at least he didn't blame us for picking this facility.

Our meeting with the administrator and head nurse went pretty well. They suggested wearing diapers to avoid the lifter, but we refused, as we had in the hospital. While we knew that option was somewhere in Mom's future, we didn't think it was time. Plus, we knew she would strongly resist.

The head nurse promised that someone would come to help Mom to the toilet within fifteen minutes of lighting the call button. They promised to investigate a mood drug to help Mom with the transition.

They seemed very concerned and polite. The administrator gave us coupons to have two meals with Mom. Since I was out of work, I offered to come and share a couple of meals with her. It would be good to sample the food anyway. We would soon be entering the busy season for the apple farm, so I was appointed.

Suddenly, I looked down at my watch and realized I had just enough time to get to my five o'clock hair appointment. Maria and John were headed to Mom's room for a visit. I had been there nearly all day, so they said goodbye.

I drove like the wind to the hairdresser's. When I made this appointment, I had a job, Mom wasn't even in the hospital, and life was somewhat normal. I had been going to Pauline for nearly ten years. She knew as much, maybe more, about me as Geoff. She cut Julie's hair and sometimes Adam's too. I thought it would be comforting and relaxing to have a haircut. Plus, I might need to look my best for job interviews, so it was important to keep this appointment, even if it meant breaking a few speed laws.

I made it just in time. The receptionist led me to Pauline's station and I sat in her comfy chair. Pauline came in with her usual smile and said, "So how are things with you today, Ms. Carrie?"

It wasn't a very difficult question. However, her words or her smile or maybe nothing at all opened the flood gates and I just started balling. I doubt if I had cried that hard since my father died. I don't even know for sure why, but I just sat in the comfy chair and cried my eyes out while poor Pauline ran for tissues. She also got me a cup of tea; and after a few drinks, I could tell her a bit about my day, my week, my messes. She was more sympathetic than anyone in my life. Of course, everyone knows hairdressers are really the best therapists. In any event, when I left, I had not only a new hairstyle, but new attitude. I left some of my grief over Mom's situation, and mine, in the hairdresser's chair, along with about a gallon of tears.

Chapter 14

Next Steps

Over the next month, my life had many changes. I was determined to maintain business working hours as much as possible, but it took a lot of self-discipline. Getting up at six a.m. when you don't have to be in an office at eight is really hard. I would manage to get up and see Adam off to school and see him when he came home, something I had been missing. I wondered what mischief he might get into if he didn't know I would be home and expecting him. I forced myself to continue my exercise routine, but nothing was coming easy.

There was so much to do to start my own company, I wasn't sure I could manage it. I would spend one day sending out resumes and the next making plans for my new company. I needed a name, a logo, equipment, and staff. At times it overwhelmed me. And then there was the issue of office space. I didn't want to bankrupt my family by renting office space with no certain income. I also knew brick-and-mortar office space would increase my prices. I found that I could work from my home successfully but was afraid of the stigma stamped on home-based companies. I doubted that I could ever get a substantial company or even Bobby Wright to commit to an agency out of my house.

I knew, in any case, if I were to start my own company, I would first have to find a professional graphic designer willing to work with an unknown upstart company. A friend gave me a great lead on a work-from-home graphic designer. So, I made an appointment and went to see her.

Her name was Marci Goldman and she lived only twenty minutes away. She wanted to meet at her house; and since I didn't have an office, that seemed fine. She greeted me in jeans and T-shirt and asked me to follow her to her conference room. I was quite impressed, a home-based business with a conference room. What next? She led me to her dining room, where she had assembled her resume, portfolio, tablets of paper, and coffee.

"Welcome to my conference room," Marci said.

A dining room as a conference room; what a brilliant idea! The table actually looked similar to the one at Ryan Advertising, without the china hutch in the corner and family pictures on the wall.

"I have one of these," I managed to say, a bit in awe.

"A dining room?" asked Marci.

"No," I smiled, "a conference room."

Suddenly I could see endless possibilities for my home office. I not only had an empty room for an office in my house, but I had a conference room too.

Marci was a very talented designer that left the craziness of the agency world after she had children. She said she was willing to work forty hours a week but that was never enough for her agency, and it was too much for her young family. The only way she could continue her design work and raise her family was to create a home-based design company. She found several clients and was doing some amazing work. She had no interest in coming to work full-time for me, but would be delighted to work on a *seamless* contract basis. That meant she would work for my clients under the banner of my company, on a project-by-project basis. She would not get a salary, but be paid for work she did.

Since I didn't have enough capital to pay her full-time, this was a perfect arrangement. Since Marci required a babysitter to go to client meetings, she was happy for me to do the contact work, and she could do the design.

I liked Marci. I liked her talent. I liked that she was a mom trying to use her talents and raise a family. I liked that she was a woman. I had had enough of working with men designers. This was very comfortable. If a talented lady like Marci was successful working from her home, surely there were other talented women in the same situation.

Paging through the many business cards I had acquired over the years, I found the names of some other talented ladies I thought could join our team. One call led to another; and before long, I had located a web designer, a bookkeeper, a publicist, a direct mail specialist, a media buyer, and phone solicitor, all willing to work on a contract basis from their homes. Now, all I needed was a name and a logo.

I spent one day on the living room floor playing with names. I used the phone book, the business journal, and the dictionary to mix and match names. I made a list of ten potential names and conducted a search on each one to determine if there were existing websites with those names. I narrowed the list to six names.

Using my new team of talented people I had interviewed as my sounding board, I sent them each a survey to gauge their views on the name. As cream rises to the top, one name surfaced above all the others. The winner was Team Marketing, with a nod to the talented team of professionals I had assembled. It took a little trip to the Secretary of State's office to register the name, and we were in business.

Marci agreed to create a logo and letterhead for a steal; and my new web designer, Debbie, would create a website. With everything in place, I began making calls to my ex-clients and anyone I knew. Soon, I was busy meeting with potential Team Marketing clients to introduce them to my new company.

While my new business was soaring off the ground, things with Mom were not as good. She hated every minute at the Garden House. True, the nursing staff was very slow to answer a page and attention to the patients' needs was below our expectations, but there were good things too.

I often came for meals with Mom. The food was good and the dining room warm and cheery. The grounds were lovely.

As soon as Mom started complaining and begging me to take her home, I pulled up the wheelchair and took her for a walk. We watched squirrels run up trees with nuts and birds build nests. We counted the blooms on an azalea bush and the water lily blooms.

I came on Sunday mornings and wheeled her to the lovely nondenominational church service. It was simple and small. After the service, they had a cookies and coffee. There were many lovely people I thought Mom could get to know, but she flatly refused to even share names. She kept saying, "I'm going home soon, so no point in getting to know people."

She refused to get her hair cut in the elder-friendly salon; she refused to play games at game time; she refused to attend the sing-along or entertainment. In short, she was so determined to not like the Garden House, she refused to enjoy anything. On the other hand, she was working hard to get better. Her mobility was improving steadily. When she had entered the Garden House, we thought she would never go home again. But now, living at home, with some help, seemed like a definite possibility.

If my visits with Mom were difficult, Maria's were heart-wrenching and John's impossible. While I was pretty good at distracting Mom from her constant pleas to go home, Maria and John found it more difficult. Maria was constantly battling the staff to improve Mom's conditions and reduce the response time. Every medical change took weeks and countless calls and paperwork to implement. It took us nearly three weeks to get Mom on a mood drug routine. We were constantly telling the staff she was agitated and needed medication, but first we had to arrange a visit with their psychologist, who was only available once a week. This made Mom furious because she thought we were trying to get her declared incompetent, and she just got angrier. Before the psychologist would write a prescription, he needed clearance from a general practitioner and cardiologist.

John just didn't have any training or patience for this. Fighting the nursing staff was beyond his capacity. He had no practice at saying "no" to Mom and was in agony over her berating him for "dumping her in this horrible place." Maria and I increased our visits so John could stay away.

My new job flexibility gave me plenty of time for visits, but it wasn't enough. In the end, she wore us down until we relented and prepared to bring her home. John had busied himself with more alterations to Mom's house so it would accommodate the wheelchair. The Garden House did its job. They taught Mom to care for herself from the wheelchair and gave her enough mobility to live on her own, with a lot of help from us.

It was a warm October day when we finally brought Mom home. John had agreed to spend the first few nights in her house to make sure she was going to be okay. We set up a portable commode in her bedroom because we knew she couldn't get to the bathroom herself at night. John had torn down the walls around the bathroom and widened the door so the wheelchair would fit. Maria was supervising the vast array of medications and doctor appointments. I was back on schedule, every Sunday, cleaning her house, washing clothes and dishes, and making Sunday dinners. Mom was thrilled to be back in her house, even with all the difficulties. Maria was thrilled that she didn't have to take so much time away from the apple store to visit Mom. John was thrilled that he could see Mom without the barrage of threats, pleas, and cries to go home. He didn't mind spending the night at Mom's because he could get an extra thirty minutes of sleep in the morning being so close to work.

I, on the other hand, missed the Garden House. I dreaded cleaning Mom's house. I never knew what disaster I would walk into each week. There might be a massive pile of dirty dishes, some had been sitting in the sink a week, or a pile of soiled clothes with urine or spit up. The dirt just seemed to pile up in Mom's house. At the Garden House, I could visit Mom without these daunting tasks. But all Mom could see was that she was in her house.

Along with Mom's diminished mobility was a diminished mental state. It was hard to tell if the massive amount of medication she was taking was affecting her brain or if something else was going on.

We continued to take Mom to the psychologist because her behavior was troubling, but she hated these visits. He suggested we see a neurologist, which led to an MRI. Of course, the MRI itself and the results were separate visits. I was selected to take Mom to the neurologist to discuss the results. It seemed we had been over this road so many times I was really not expecting anything. I was prepared for another incomplete diagnosis with no real news, so I sat rather uninterested as Dr. Midland began to talk. I noticed he was actually speaking to me as if Mom was not in the room.

"I understand your mother has had some behavior change of the last year or so; is that correct?"

"Well, yes, I suppose," I answered.

While I had often discussed this with Maria and John and, frankly, everybody I knew, I had never discussed it with Mom in the room.

"You can see in this MRI," he began, pointing to an X-ray, "brain damage caused by a minor stroke; but it's been some time ago, maybe years ago. I can't tell when or how severe the damage was. Can you tell me when this event happened and what your doctor did at the time?"

My mouth was wide open, but no words came out. My mother did have a stroke, certainly not years ago. He must have some other mom's MRI. Then she spoke—the silent, ignored voice in the room.

"Yeah, I know something happened back when. My doctor is retired now, you know, but he could tell you," she said.

This was more shocking than the doctor's pronouncement.

"Mom, why didn't you tell us?" I asked in stunned disbelief.

"Well, Dr. Fitz said there wasn't anything he could do to change it. He said if I told you I might end up in a nursing home, so we let it pass."

"Actually," said Dr. Midland, "there are a lot of things you can do to improve the chance of future strokes and regain some lost mental ability. But since there's been so much time, I can't do anything now. However, it's quite possible that she may have had or will have mini-strokes. These are small events that often go unnoticed. They might manifest in very bizarre dreams or behavior. I see by her medication list she's already taking blood thinners and blood pressure medications. Anything I could give her now would only worsen those conditions."

"So, you're telling me," I said with a huge lump in my throat, "that Mom first suffered a stroke years ago and may again, but you can't do anything else for her?"

"Not in her current condition," he affirmed. "But if another significant event takes place, you should be sure to contact me immediately."

I got up to leave then sat back down again, remembering why I came in the first place. "What about the anxiety drugs Mom's taking?" I asked.

"I doubt that they will do any good," he said, "or any harm," he quickly added. "Brain damage is not repairable with drugs. Read the side effects carefully. If you notice any of them, I'd suggest stop taking the drug. It won't do that much to help her, but I don't suppose it hurts to try."

We drove back in silence. I was glad for the silence because I had much to absorb. But this was always Mom's way of avoiding a difficult situation. It dawned on me that this was how she handled every difficult situation: Dad's cancer, Dad's massive stroke, Dad's death. "Let's just not talk about it and it will all be better," she'd say. However, not talking never made anything better. Maybe that's why I tend to overtalk everything. I'm trying to make up for all the things Mom didn't talk about when I was young. Maybe that's why she keeps diverting my efforts to continue our talks about her past.

The next chapter is the one she has never discussed with anyone. It's the most painful chapter. It's about Dad's illness and passing. I was now determined to force this discussion before it was too late.

When I dropped Mom off, she was very tired and I helped her into bed for a nap. I walked over to the apple store for a talk with Maria. She was busy at the cash register.

"So, how did the neurologist visit go?" she asked. "Another dead end? I told you she didn't have Alzheimer's."

"No, she doesn't have Alzheimer's, but we do need to talk. I'd like to have a family meeting with you and John."

She stopped her work and her cheerful customer face disappeared.

"Something's wrong, isn't it?" she said solemnly.

"It's not all that bad, but I'd rather talk to you and John at the same time."

"How about tomorrow evening?" she suggested. "I'll tell John."

"Okay. Tomorrow, your house."

The time for our meeting came slowly. I couldn't concentrate on work. I was thinking how to tell them the doctor we had entrusted our mother with knew she had a stroke years ago and just did nothing. Not only that, but Mom knew and chose not to tell us. Every time I thought about it, I just got angrier and angrier. I wasn't sure I could get this all out without the anger exploding.

Sitting around Maria's dining room table, I told my siblings what the doctor said. Maria had tears in her eyes. She never trusted Dr. Fitz and had tried to get Mom to change years ago. But Mom had gone to him for nearly thirty years. We suspected she should have had, could have had the gallbladder surgery years ago, but for Dr. Fitz's negligence. We even thought he first saw the signs of congestive heart failure, but chose to ignore it. He may have figured she would soon die anyway, so why treat it. Maria's mind was in the same place.

"I think when Mom first got congestive heart failure, Dr. Fitz knew it and sent her home to die," Maria finally said. It was what I was thinking.

"That son of a bitch," John swore.

I looked up sharply. I had never heard John swear like that.

"Things are going to continue to change, and not for the better."

"I still think Mom can walk again," Maria stated. "Dr. Benson from the Garden House said we should take Mom to physical therapy to continue her therapy."

"How many doctors can we take her to?" I asked. "I want her to have good care, but we need to be realistic."

"If being realistic means accepting that Mom isn't going to walk and is losing her mind, then I vote for hope," Maria argued.

"I believe in hope too. But hope where no medical science can support it, that's not realistic. How long can we continue to provide all her care? I know she thinks she wants to stay in that house, but at what cost? How long can we do this? I've already lost a job."

"And do you think you are worse off for losing that miserable job?" Maria asked, much too sharply.

I had no answer. I just starred at Maria with glassy eyes. I knew bringing up the job was the wrong move. It just slipped out.

"I think we're letting emotions get carried away. This is hard enough without us bickering," said John, ever the peacemaker. "Listen, I was a lot younger than you two when Dad died and Mom was everything to me. I can't put a price or limit on what I owe her. If she wants to stay in that damn house, then that's what's going to happen. That's all there is to it."

"Do you think the mom who worked so hard for us after Dad died would want Maria to cripple herself bathing her? Or John to give up any hope of a personal life to live with her?" I asked in frustration.

"Carrie, you do what you have to do," John said. "Maria and I are going to keep Mom in her house, with you or without you. That's just the way it is."

I had no answer. There was an ocean of tears pushing hard to explode out of my reddened eyes and I didn't want them to see it. I loved my life, my husband, and children. I desperately wanted to make my new company succeed, partly for vindictive reasons. I knew, in my heart, that most of the reasons I didn't want to keep Mom in her house were selfish, but so what? I couldn't make any of this come out without hurting these people whom I love so dearly, so I did the next most hurtful thing. I got up and left.

I jumped in my car and pulled off without even a goodbye. As soon as I got in the car, the tears exploded out. I was crying so hard I could hardly see to drive. I pulled over at the first gas station and sat there and sobbed. When the flood subsided a little, I drove home. By the time I got home, Geoff was already in bed. He sat up when I crawled into bed.

"How did it go at Maria's house?" he asked.

"Awful. They are determined to keep Mom at home even if it kills us all."

"I'm sorry. My mom called tonight. She wants us to come to Kansas City this weekend."

"Can't you see I'm upset?" I snapped. "I don't want to talk about anything."

"Okay," Geoff said sharply. "We'll talk tomorrow."

Now, I had managed to alienate the last person in the whole world who still loved me. And another flood of tears burst out.

The next morning, I was still feeling sore at the world, so I stayed in bed until Geoff had gone to work. I had a ton of paperwork to do, so I got dressed and started working in my office. I was deep in QuickBooks training when Geoff called.

"I'm really sorry about your mom, but I need to talk about my mom."

"I'm really sorry too," I said sincerely. "This whole thing has made me a first-class bitch."

There was a moment of silence when I suspect Geoff was trying to figure out the best thing to say. His better/smarter side won and let it pass. I suspected his tongue was bleeding.

"My mother wants the whole family, me, George, and Tom, to come to Kansas City this weekend. She says she has something important to tell us and doesn't want to do it over the phone."

"Wow, that's pretty big. Do you have any idea what she wants?"

"No," said Geoff, "but she's never asked us to come like this before, so I think we need to go."

"It's really, really bad timing. I've got all this stuff with my mom, and I'm trying to get a business started. Can you go without me?"

"I could, but I don't want to," Geoff answered. "I know you've had a ton of stress lately, maybe this will be fun, a weekend away together. Come with me, please."

Geoff could have said a lot of things. He could have said, *You owe me this because of all the crap I've put up with because of your mom.* He could have said, *You've spent so much time with your mom, how about one lousy weekend with mine.* He could have said, *You should be glad I want you with me at all after the way you've been acting.* But he said the one word I couldn't refuse. He said, "Please."

"Okay, I'll go," I told him.

Chapter 15

The Other Mother

After I had thought about it for a while, I knew getting out of town for a few days was the best thing for me. I called Maria at a time I knew she wouldn't answer to leave a message on her phone that Geoff and I were going to Kansas City for a few days. I sent out emails to all my business partners and anyone I thought might be contacting me that I would be out of town for a few days. It seemed very professional to be out of town, I thought. Maybe they'll think I'm on a business trip.

When I started packing, I was really happy to be leaving. We always had a good time in Kansas City. It was only a four-hour drive, but we seldom went. Geoff wasn't quite as close with his family as I was. Maybe they were just more independent, but it was good to be going somewhere. We often stayed with Geoff's mom when we went, but this time we made reservation at a hotel near her home, to make it even more special and private.

The drive to Kansas City was very pleasant. We were curious about the reason for the summons, but not so curious to prevent us from enjoying the trip.

Phyllis Young was only a couple of years younger than my mother, but much more active. She had had a difficult life, but had survived well and was enjoying retirement.

Geoff's family owned a business like mine. They had a small hardware store in a suburb of Kansas City. It was a meeting place when Geoff was young. His father was loved by everyone, and the whole town stopped by for advice on almost everything. Phyllis was the bookkeeper. She had worked long hours trying to keep the business afloat.

One day, after she had turned sixty, she woke up and told Geoff's dad, Tom Sr., she didn't want to work anymore and he should sell the business. So, he did. He got enough for a comfortable, if not luxurious, retirement. But shortly after they sold the hardware store, he began having problems. First, he had prostate cancer, then emphysema, then a crippling stroke. He died nearly ten years ago from complications of the stroke. Phyllis had to put him in a nursing home after the stroke. It was very hard on her. It took much of their savings. She was determined to visit every day, and every day he begged to go home. Like my mom, she had decided to stay in her house after Tom died.

Geoff's younger brother, George, lived close by and would help with some home repair and maintenance, but he had his own family and didn't have a lot of time to spend helping her. Tom Jr. lived in New Jersey and seldom came to Kansas City. He was a financial wizard and never took time off. I was quite surprised that he was coming. This would be the first meeting of all three brothers in many years. I think Geoff was looking forward to it.

We pulled into the hotel around lunchtime and decided not to tell anyone we were in town until after we checked in and had a few romantic moments together. We finally arrived at Geoff's mom's house around three p.m., looking much too happy to be coming to a serious family meeting.

Phyllis was very old school. Like my family, food always came first. The first order of business, after all the greetings were over, was to decide on a restaurant and make dinner reservations. Then we all collected in the living room for her to make her announcement.

She first said everything was fine and she was in good health, then added, "I've made a decision about my life I need to share with you. I've watched many of my friends and family fighting to stay in their homes. I see their kids struggling to keep up an old house and old parents. It's a terrible strain on a family. Tom and Geoff live so far away, and George has enough to handle with his own family. None of you need to work on this old place. I don't want to be a burden on my family. I know we all say that, but I'm going to do something about it. I'm selling this old house, while it's still standing, and moving into a retirement center. I've picked a place that can provide assisted living or skilled nursing care should I ever need that. Look, who am I kidding, everybody needs that at some point. While I still have my mind and mobility intact, I'm going to make the move. I want you all to see the place I've picked out and support my decision."

Tom, Geoff, and George were tongue-tied. Men seldom have the right words at a time like this. But I always have words. Phyllis just said the words I had desperately wanted to hear my mother say for the last five years. I knew I'd never hear this from my mother, but was so very grateful to Phyllis for this gift.

I ran to her and gave her a big hug. I whispered in her ear, "Thank you, Mom, thank you."

She smiled and patted my head.

Eventually, Geoff and his brothers came around to the idea. At first there were discussions. Tom thought it was a bad time to sell a house; George argued that he could do a better job of taking care of the old house. I suspect he took this announcement as a condemnation of his ability to maintain the house. None of them had been through the process of taking care of a disabled parent or knew what staying at home would mean. But once we saw the retirement village, everyone changed their minds.

Phyllis had picked a lovely new facility in the suburbs that was completely contained. It offered independent living where Phyllis would live, assisted living, and the complex also offered skilled nursing care. Should Phyllis's health decline, she could move into a more appropriate section. She would have a villa townhome that was, basically, a one-bedroom apartment. It was very small, but very well designed. She showed us how she planned to decorate and furnish her new home. When she talked about what she would put where, her eyes lit up. She said she was getting a new flowered sofa to put in the small living room.

"You know, Tom hated anything flowered," she said, "so I'm going to get everything with big flowers." She giggled a little, turned to me, and added, "You know, I feel like a new bride."

I gave her a big hug and said, "I'm so very proud of you. You deserve this."

"This is my gift to myself for living so long," Phyllis said. "This is going to be my home. All mine. I don't have to consider anybody else's opinion. It's very exciting."

The ride back to St. Louis was long and very quiet. I think Geoff was having trouble processing the whole thing.

Finally, I broke the silence. "I'm so proud of your mother. She's taken control of her life and found a way to take care of herself without depending on her family. I can't imagine how we would manage two parents who needed as much help as my mom."

"You think so?" Geoff asked. "I'm thinking she just doesn't want us in her life. Or, maybe she thinks we don't want to take care of her. That's not true, you know. I was certainly not looking forward to taking care of her, but we would have found a way. This is going to cost her most of her savings. What if she runs out of money? Then what? I just think she should have talked it over with us before she made such a big decision. I'm not even certain she's capable of making such a big decision by herself. I wonder if we could have her declared incompetent."

"Geoff, I can't understand why you're not thrilled about this. Your mom is much more capable of making this decision than you think. I understand you would have liked to be consulted, but this *is* a good thing. It's so much better than my mom's situation."

"You can't compare it to your mom," Geoff said with growing anger. "They're much different people. My mom would never demand so much or need so much help. If she did, we could make the move then. Not now. It's too soon. My mom *is* not your mom."

The rest of the ride home was deathly silent. Geoff needed to come to terms with his mom's decision. She didn't need his wise counsel for this last great decision and that hurt him. Nothing I said would make any difference.

Chapter 16
Making Peace

By the time we got home, I had decided the best thing for me was to concentrate on my new business and avoid everybody in my family. I had a talk with Julie and told her about Grandma Young's decision. Julie thought it was a great idea. I carefully skipped the part about her dad not being too happy with the decision or our argument. I also avoided telling her about my tiff with my siblings. I just didn't want to reveal what a troublesome person her mom had become.

I needed some advice and someone to talk to who didn't have an opinion, so I called my friend, Joan. She agreed to meet me for dinner, and I knew Geoff wouldn't mind. I don't think he was really eager to see me just now anyway.

Joan was a great listener. Maybe the best I've ever known. She could spend the whole evening asking questions about you and you'd go home thinking you had a great conversation; but later, you'd realize you never heard one single thing about her life. We've been friends for nearly twenty years, and I've learned over the years that I need to ask about her life or I'll make the whole evening about me. As great as that sounds, it always comes with regret and it's not the friend I want to be. Joan is a brilliant business woman and knowledgeable about almost any subject. She has an interesting perspective on everything from art to politics. I don't want to miss her views, even though the temptation to thoroughly explore all my issues is hard to resist.

One of Joan's many talents is knowing the latest trend in restaurants, so I always let her pick and I'm never disappointed. We met at the very trendy Harvest Moon, featuring everything local, from beans to buffalo. I picked a fish that was certainly not local, but this was St. Louis. Anything local would come from the Mississippi and be inedible.

Once I got talking, I just exploded. All the anger I had been concealing, about my siblings, my mother, Geoff's mother, just poured out like volcanic ash. I erupted all through cocktails, salad, and the main course, completely forgetting my vow to listen to Joan too. Suddenly, like a raging storm that had consumed itself, I was done. My fish was half eaten, but I was exhausted. I didn't even have the energy left to finish my dinner. I felt like a mop that had been squeezed dry of every last drop of moisture. All the dirt had spilled out. Nothing was left. I sat back in my chair, put my fork down, and let out a long breath.

"That was a lot," said Joan. "A lot of information, a lot of anger, a lot of issues. How did you ever hold all that in?" She smiled one those smiles that makes the world right.

I smiled back, took a long drink of wine, and a long breath and said, "You know, Joan, I came here tonight firmly resolved to listen to you and not burden you with all my stuff."

"How's that working for you?" She smiled. "You obviously needed to get all that out before you exploded, for real. You know, there are no answers for you. Nobody has a magic solution that will make all this better. It is what it is. I can only tell you two things. First, I know as surely as I know my own name that only God can give you the peace of mind you seek. You won't find it in anything in this world. Only God has the peace of mind that surpasses understanding. And in Christ is true acceptance and forgiveness. Follow Christ and you can forgive anything, even though you don't understand. There is evil in the world too. Much of our sorrow and trouble comes from him who would destroy us and keep us away from God. Don't let him in. Don't let him take control.

God does not make all things happen, but He can make all things work to your good if you let Him."

Joan was quiet for a long minute as she gave me the chance to absorb what she had said. Then she added one more point that made me very ashamed.

"I can only imagine how difficult it is to disagree with your sister and brother and husband. I say 'I can only imagine' because I have none of those. When my mother was ill, I had to make all the decisions, do everything for her. I had no one to share the burden, no one to take some of the load, no one to disagree with. I would have loved to share this grief with someone who knew our history; someone who loved her as I did. But it was just me; all me.

"I lost my mother-in-law in my divorce many years ago. I never stopped loving her, but I was no longer part of her family. When she got ill, I desperately wanted to help care for her, but it was inappropriate. I had to keep quiet and watch her decline from a distance. It was very hard.

"So, unfortunately, I can't quite understand your situation. I'm sure it must be very, very hard. I wish I could empathize more, but I can't."

Now, for the first time this evening, I had tears in my eyes. I know all this about Joan, but I could only think of me. There wasn't much left for me to say.

"You are such a dear friend, Joan," I managed to choke out. "I've been a horrible, self-absorbed skunk. You've helped me immeasurably. Maybe you were the answer to my prayers. I needed your reality check. Please let me take you out to dinner another time and, I promise, we will talk only about you. I do want to know what is going on in your family."

"That sounds like a lovely plan," said Joan smiling. "I'd love to have a *me* evening."

We made a date for two weeks.

We had another lovely evening, and I did listen. I was lucky to have family, even when they drove me mad. At least I had loved ones to travel through life with. Joan was so alone. But her steadfast faith impressed me even more. With all her trials, it seemed a miracle that her faith was so strong. But I guess that's what faith is all about, miracles.

While I had continued my Sunday dinners with Mom, I was carefully avoiding Maria and John. I cleaned the house, did her laundry, left meals for the week, and managed to have a pleasant time with Mom without seeing either of them for a few weeks. I was thinking it might take a miracle for me to make peace with Maria and John. Then my *miracle* struck.

My female problems where growing. I was hoping for menopause, but that's not the miracle I got. I had very heavy vaginal bleeding with increased frequency and intensity. While worrying about Mom, I had tried to ignore this, but it was getting way out of hand. I decided it was time for a visit with my ob-gyn, Dr. Hughes.

I made the appointment and told him my problems. He conducted the usual exam.

"It appears you have some kind of growth in your uterus," he said like he was just saying, *So, how's your love life?* Then he added, "We'll have to take a closer look at this. Jenna will take a sonogram for me. Let's see what it looks like."

Well, I thought, it's not going to look like the Mona Lisa. I'm sure of that.

I followed expressionless Jenna to the sonogram room. My mind was racing. After the sonogram, Jenna directed me to the doctor's office. As I waited for him to return, I studied everything in the room: the diplomas, the charts, the pharmaceutical ads. I wondered, *Is this the room where he gives bad news?*

He returned twenty minutes later with a file and another nurse.

"Carrie," Dr. Hughes began.

He had called me by my first name. He never uses my first name. This can't be good.

"You have a growth in your uterus about the size of a plum. It's not huge, which is why it hasn't caused much pain, but it has to come out. Would next Thursday be convenient?"

"Next Thursday? Convenient for what?" I asked, stunned. I guess I knew the answer, but I needed to hear him say it.

"To come to the hospital to remove the growth," he answered. "It's a simple procedure. It may require one-night stay in the hospital, but shouldn't be more than that."

I felt like I was in an episode of *Grey's Anatomy*, but those people always had serious illnesses. That can't be what I have. Sure, I can come to the hospital, but that's not the important question. The better question is, why?

He seemed to be avoiding the proverbial elephant in the room, the big word. Might as well get it out on the table, I thought. It looks like he's side stepping the bigger issue.

"Do you think I might have cancer?" I managed to spit out.

"It's not likely," he began, "but I can't rule it out either. Cancer tumors don't often look like this. We will go in and remove the lump. If we don't like the way it looks, we'll do a full hysterectomy. Then we'll evaluate from there. Is Thursday okay?"

"Thursday is fine," I replied.

Of course, Thursday wasn't fine. I wasn't ready to have a hysterectomy or have anything else, for that matter, removed on Thursday. There was so much more I wanted to say.

When I was back in my car, I couldn't remember a thing I had said. I looked down at the pile of paper I held in my hand. My world was tumbling right in front of me, and I couldn't seem to find the way out of the doctor's parking lot. I needed to talk to someone. I needed my sister. I needed Maria. But I was mad at her. I didn't even know if she wanted to talk to me. Why on earth did I let this thing go so long. Now, when I needed her, things were too awkward. I took a deep breath and started the car. First, I needed ice cream.

I found the closest Dairy Queen and got a shake to go.

With the help of my happy drug, a Dairy Queen chocolate malted, I made it home and sat for a bit looking at the phone. I picked it up and dialed. Maria answered on the first ring.

"Carrie, I'm so glad to hear from you," she said. "I was just going to call. I'm taking Mom into the hospital. I think something's wrong. Do you want to meet me there?"

"Sure, I'm on my way," I replied. I didn't even bother asking any questions. If Maria thought Mom needed to go to the hospital, I'm sure she did. It just wasn't my day for asking too many questions. My news was going to wait. Just as well. I didn't have the energy for it now.

On the way to the hospital, I wanted to get more ice cream, but I realized no amount of chocolate malts would fix this day. What I needed was to talk with God. In all this miserable day, I hadn't made time for God. I often prayed in my car and all sorts of places, but today, I wanted to talk to God in his place. Fortunately, the church was more or less on the way to the hospital. I thought I'd just stop for a short chat.

I pulled into the parking lot. I knew the front door would be locked, but I found a side door and stepped in. It was quiet. I sat in a front row pew. I just sat silently looking at the huge cross and magnificent stained-glass windows on the altar. I never noticed how beautiful they were before. Maybe I hadn't seen them in the fading afternoon light, or maybe I had not seen them with such a heavy heart before. They seemed to gleam. It felt that Jesus was staring right at me. So, I just started talking to him.

"I wish you could tell me why all this stuff is happening? I've been good, haven't I? After all, I teach Sunday School. That should get me something, shouldn't it? I know I can't get special treatment for doing good, but I don't deserve all this trouble. And now cancer? Really, why would you give me, of all people, cancer? Can't you see I have way too much on my plate for cancer? Who's going to help take care of Mom if I can't? While we're on the subject, why would you give her so much pain? She has devoted her whole life to you. She's never done a single bad thing. And look what you've done to Maria. She's better than both of us and now she has the huge burden of taking care of Mom with a failing business. Yeah, that's another thing. Couldn't you help out the apple farm just a little? You do have control of weather and crops. You could at the very least see they have a good crop and a good market so they don't struggle so much. What about one of those famous miracles? Would that be so hard? Of all the people in the world getting rich, why not us?"

Suddenly my anger and frustration spilled over and I picked up the pew Bible and threw it at the altar.

"I don't want to have cancer," I screamed and threw another pew Bible.

"I don't want to see my mom hurting," I screamed again, threw another Bible.

"I don't want to have to take care of my mom," I shouted even louder, hurling a third Bible, picking up another.

"Careful, we have a limited supply of those" came a voice from the back of the church. I jumped and put down the *weapon* in my hand.

"Why are you so angry at God, Carrie?" It was Pastor Mueller. His voice was calm and gentle. It quieted my rage.

"I didn't know anyone was here," I answered, embarrassed.

"That, I gathered," said Pastor Mueller, smiling.

"Oh, that," I was looking at my shoes. "I was just letting off some steam."

"That was a lot of steam. Do you want to talk about it?"

"I don't know," I hesitated. "I was just being selfish, I guess. It seems like God's not listening to me."

"You think throwing Bibles will change that?" he asked.

"Oh, so sorry. I'll pick them up."

"Why don't you tell me why you were throwing Bibles first," he said taking a seat across the aisle from me.

"My mom is back in the hospital and I don't want to have to worry about her and spend so much time taking care of her and…"

Suddenly there were tears and I couldn't finish.

"And," he said gently.

"And I've got cancer," I blurted sniffling. "Or I might have cancer of the uterus. I have to have surgery next Thursday to find out. I don't want to have surgery. I don't want to have cancer."

"That is a lot. I'm so sorry," he said gently. "And you blame God for all this?"

"Well, I don't understand why he's doing this to us. I mean, we're not bad people. Look at all the time I give teaching Sunday School and how devoted my mom was all those years."

"I think you know the answer." Pastor Mueller said. "You're a good Sunday School teacher, Carrie. I bet you've even taught about the blind man. You know the story, when Jesus was asked who sinned to make the man blind, and He answered, 'No one.'"

He paused a second while I remembered the story. Then he continued.

"And I bet you've told your class, 'God doesn't cause all trouble, but he can make all trouble to work to his glory.'"

"I know, I know," I was looking at my shoes again. "But today, when the doctor said I could have cancer, then Maria said she was taking Mom to the hospital, it just all seemed like words. It didn't help."

"Whom have you told about your medical problems?" he asked. Somehow, I thought he knew the answer.

"No one, yet. I didn't get the chance before the second shoe dropped, I was going to talk to God about it, that's why I came in here but, well, the conversation kind of got out of hand."

"I'd say it was a pretty one-sided conversation, wouldn't you?"

"Well, yeah, but I *was* talking to God. It's kind of hard to get Him to talk back."

"Most people have a lot of trouble with that. Not because God doesn't talk to us, but because we're not very good at listening. He does a lot of His talking in those Bibles you were slinging."

"Oh, so sorry about that." My shoes got ever more interesting.

"Get me one of those Bibles, and I'll show you how God talks to you."

A little confused, I picked up a Bible and brought it to him. He opened it and said, "There was a man in the Bible who had a lot of trouble. He lost all his children in a terrible storm. Then he lost all his possessions, then his health, and he asked God why. Do you know whom I'm talking about?"

"Job," I answered.

"Yes, Job. And do you know what God answered when Job finally got fed up and lashed out at God?"

"No, I guess not," I said softly.

"Let me read it to you," Pastor Mueller said. "God said to Job, 'Where were you when I laid the earth's foundation? Who marked off its dimensions while the morning stars sang together and all the angels shouted for joy? Do you know when the mountain goats give birth? Do you watch when the doe bears her fawn? Do you count the months 'til they bear? Does the eagle soar at your command and build his nest on high? Do you have an arm like God's and can your voice thunder like this?'"

"Then what did Job say?" I asked.

"He said," replied Pastor Mueller, "'I know that you can do all things, no plan of yours can be thwarted. Surely, I spoke of things I did not understand, things too wonderful for me to know.'"

"That's not really an answer"

"That's God's answer," said Pastor Mueller. "Basically, I think He said to Job, 'I am God, and I know what I'm doing. It's not your place to questions me.' God doesn't always tell us what He's doing or why, but He is still God and he cares deeply for us. He cares so much about what happens here on earth, he knows when the mountain goat bears her young and the eagle soars. Surely, he knows about your situation, and he loves you and cares for you."

"I do know that. I'm just weak," I said, now looking at Pastor Mueller instead of my shoes.

"And so are we all," he replied. "Would you like to pray with me?"

We prayed together, sincerely. Then I returned the Bibles and got a new candle and headed for St. Mark's Hospital. I left behind much of my anger and came out calmer than I had been in a long time.

I found Maria and John with Mom in the emergency room. Mom was resting in one of the ER-bay beds, and Maria and John were talking quietly. When they saw me, they jumped up and left the room. I could tell by their face's things were bad.

"What happened?" I asked.

"I'm not sure," Maria answered. "I came into the house to check on her and she was on the floor unconscious. She had fallen out of the wheelchair, but I don't think that's why she was unconscious. I called 911 and then John. She had come to before they arrived, but she's very foggy, mentally. We're just waiting to see what the doctor says."

"Have you been able to talk with her at all?" I asked.

"Just a little," Maria said. "She knew me and John, but not much else."

We returned to her little cubby with barely room for three chairs. There wasn't much left to say, a word here or there. Nothing seemed very important. I asked about the apple store. They answered briefly. They asked about my business. I answered briefly. We watched Mom sleeping. We waited.

Finally, Dr. Midland came in the room. He said he wanted to talk with us and directed us to a small waiting area.

"We think your mom has had a stroke," he said. "It's not a major event, but in her condition, it is significant. We won't know much for a couple of days, so I'd rather not speculate. My best guess is she will recover enough to sit in the wheelchair, but she will need a lot of care."

"When will you know more?" asked Maria.

"In a couple of days," said Dr. Midland. "We can talk more then." And he left.

The room was deadly quiet. We didn't know what to say. The three of us sat in silence at least thirty minutes. We were each lost in our own thoughts. There were no tears. We had passed that point long ago. There were no debates. We were all argued out. We just sat feeling each other's presence and glad to have each other to share our silence.

"Your mom is awake."

We all jumped at the nurse breaking our coveted silence. In unison, we got up and went to her room.

Maria bent close to Mom. "How are you feeling?" she asked.

"Where am I?" Mom replied. "I'm very tired. Is this my bed? How come you are here?"

John answered her when Maria's voice failed.

"You're in the hospital, Mom," he said gently. "You got sick and we brought you here."

"Well, I just need some rest," she answered. "You didn't need to take me to the hospital just for getting sick. That's a lot of bother," she chided. "I want to go home now."

"The doctor thinks you need to be here a few days," said Maria finding her voice. There's nothing like a good chiding from Mom to help you find your voice.

"We're going to make sure they take good care of you here," I told her, scraping the bottom of the barrel for a comment.

"Who was that?" Mom asked.

I thought the answer should be, *Your least favorite child,* but fortunately I had had that talk with God.

"It's Carrie, Mom," Maria said gently.

"Oh. The light's not so good in here." As if she needed an excuse for not recognizing her own child.

"I'm tired. I think I want to sleep." And with that, she fell back asleep.

By ten p.m. Mom was in a room and again sleeping soundly. We agreed she would be fine by herself in the hospital until morning. We worked out a plan for sharing the visiting time the next two days. I offered to take the early shift tomorrow, and Maria and John would follow, filling out the day. I was much too tired and emotionally drained to mention my *problem*. After a round of hugs, we walked silently to our cars.

It had been a very long day; but somehow, I knew it wouldn't be the longest day in the coming months. It was clear to me, if not Maria and John, that Mom's condition would continue to decline to the inevitable. Mom's time on earth was very limited. As hard as it was to face this most inconvenient truth, there was no denying it now. The other truth I had to face was that I was done arguing with John and Maria. Whatever they wanted—for however long it took—that, we would do.

When I crawled into bed, Geoff was sound asleep. For once, this was a relief. I didn't have the energy to talk to Geoff about any of the day's events. I just wanted to sleep. This, God granted me.

My alarm rang at 5:30. I got up and quickly showered. I had just enough time to tell Geoff I was off to the hospital. This was such a common routine now that it didn't need any explanation. He recognized better than we did what it meant—another in a long string of episodes leading to the end of Mom's life.

There was another conversation I desperately needed to have with Geoff about my impending surgery. I knew he would be furious that I waited so long to tell him, but what else could I do? I couldn't tell him on the phone or after he was asleep or before he woke up. What was left? Before I left, I told him I wanted to talk over dinner tonight. He sleepily said, "Okay." Then I left.

Mom was sitting up, drinking her water when I entered her room.

"Hi, Mom. How are you today?"

"Well, I feel okay, I guess, but I'm in the hospital. Do you know why I'm here? Did I fall out of the wheelchair?" she asked.

I didn't know what to say. We hadn't discussed how we would tell her or what we would say. I didn't want to be the one to tell her she had had a stroke. I wasn't sure how she'd take it. Maria was so much better with these things than me.

"It was something like that. Maria found you on the floor."

"Well, why didn't she just put me back in the chair?" she asked.

"You were unconscious," I said, growing more uncomfortable with the conversation. How many ways can you sidestep an important issue? I thought. But then, it wasn't like I was talking to someone who had a full deck.

"I don't remember that," Mom said.

"I think that happens when you're unconscious," I told her..

"You'd think I'd remember something like that, wouldn't you?" she continued. "All I know is I woke up this morning in this hospital. I don't even know how I got here. I wish Maria was here. Didn't she bring me?"

"An ambulance brought you, Mom. Maria found you and called the ambulance. She told you in the emergency room last night. Don't you remember?" I asked.

What a dumb question. Of course, she doesn't remember. She wouldn't be talking like this if she did.

"Can you tell me, what was the last thing you remember?" I asked, reaching for a new subject.

"I don't know what the last thing was I remember," she said, looking very confused. Then just out of the blue, she added, "You're married, aren't you?"

"Yes, Mom. My husband is Geoff." A little sniff escaped.

"Geoff, yes, I remember. He's a good guy. And you have children, don't you?"

This was almost too much to bear. How could Mom forget her grandchildren? How would I tell them?

"Yes, Mom, I have two, Julie and Adam. Julie's in college. Do you remember them?"

"Julie and Adam, sounds very familiar. Yes, I think I do remember them."

Just then the doctor came in.

"Well, Mrs. Schmidt, I have some good news. You had a mild stroke. We don't think it was a major stroke. We're going to keep you here for a couple of days to make sure. But I don't think you'll be able to take care of yourself when you leave. You should talk about that with your daughter."

"This is my daughter Carrie," Mom told the doctor. "She has two children. Imagine that. She was born in this hospital, you know."

The doctor smiled. He saw the anguished look on my face and understood. A piece of my mother had disappeared with the stroke. He asked to see me in the hall.

"I can have a social worker come and talk to you about your options."

"Options?" I repeated in a fog.

"I understand that this is difficult," he continued. "I don't think your mother will recover from this episode. I think it's time to consider a nursing home. But you will have to make some provisions for your mother's care before we can release her. It may take a few days, so I suggest you look at your options as soon as possible. Here is the number for the people you should talk to. You'll need to make an appointment as soon as possible."

He handed me the card and walked off.

Somewhere in what he said was a ticking bomb: nursing home. What an awful word. Did he mean she was dying? I had to find a chair, quickly. I stumbled back into the room and sat next to Mom.

"The doctor said I had a stroke," she began. "Just like Daddy. He had a stroke. But he couldn't talk or walk or use his hand. I'm not like that. I feel fine."

"Well, there are different kinds of strokes. Yours was a little one."

"An episode," she smiled. "Dr. Fitz used to call them 'episodes.' I guess that was so I didn't worry about them."

Dr. Fitz, I wish I'd never heard his name. He should have treated her for these episodes and called them "strokes."

Before I had time to think too much, Mom's breakfast came. I used the opportunity to step into the waiting room and make some calls. First, I called the number Dr. Midland gave me and made an appointment for three o'clock that afternoon. Then I called Maria and John to let them know.

When I finished, I looked around the room. It was a very pleasant space in a not-so-pleasant place. The colors were bright and cheerful. There were phones and outlets for electronic devices. There were two small sofas, several cushioned chairs, and a round table surrounded by chairs.

I sat and watched as some other people were making difficult calls to family members. One was laughing over something said on the other end of the call. Good, I thought, you should make each other laugh at a time like this. Maybe her loved one was sure to recover.

Another person was arguing with someone. They were obviously not seeing eye to eye on someone's care. I could tell this lady wanted to be anywhere else but in this all-too-cliché-ish waiting room. She was well-dressed, looked like she could be a professional, maybe a lawyer. She was in a hurry, didn't have time for illness or death.

Then there was a man dressed very casually. It looked like he had just thrown on some clothes after an urgent call. He was quiet. He was too quiet. I wondered, Did he not have anyone to talk with? Maybe there was no one else to help him make his decision. Maybe this decision, this situation, was too much, too hard for tears. Maybe he was searching for the words he needed to tell someone the awful news.

And then I thought, There are waiting rooms like this all over the city, all over the country, all over the world. Sickness and death come to every family, to every one of us. What separates us four in this hospital waiting room? In a sense, we are all here waiting for life and death news, waiting for someone to die.

What separates me is that I know, with as much certainty as I know the sun will rise tomorrow, that my mother's suffering will end soon, and she will have the joy of meeting her Savior face to face. I have the comfort of knowing my mother is a believer and she will be in paradise soon. While we will miss her terribly, we have the comfort that truly surpasses understanding. I have hope and I have faith.

With a renewed spirit, I went back to Mom's room. She had finished breakfast and was in good spirits.

"I was thinking about Daddy," she said smiling. She often referred to our father as "Daddy"; he called her "Mom."

"I guess I think about him a lot these days. It was so long ago that he passed. Sometimes I have trouble remembering just what he looked like. He was always so distinguished, even when he was knee-deep in mud, planting trees. He had a stroke because he had cancer. Do I have cancer?"

"No, Mom, you don't have cancer. Dad's stroke was different."

"He died from it though," she said thoughtfully. "Will I die?"

"The doctor hasn't said that," I answered as honestly as possible.

"It was awful when Daddy died," Mom said. "You kids had no idea. It was my decision to take him home after the stroke. The doctor thought I should put him in a nursing home. But I couldn't do that. It wouldn't have changed anything. I suppose it would have been easier, but we would be running to the home all the time. And where on earth would I have found the money? I was working night and day to keep the business alive. The doctor told me the best thing would be to let him go, just not call an ambulance until after he was gone. That last night was horrible. I heard the death rattle and knew the end was near. When he was finally quiet, I called the doctor."

There were tears in her eyes now. Mine too. In all these years, she had never said these things to me, or I suppose, to anyone. This must be very hard for her. I desperately wanted to say something comforting, but couldn't get the words out.

"You made me go to school that day," I finally spilled out.

"Thank you for that," she said. "I didn't know what else to do. I couldn't have the hearse come and take Daddy away with all you kids watching. It was so much easier to tell John when he came home from school. It was all so hard. I just didn't know what to do."

"It's okay." I had been waiting thirty years to hear her apologize for that terrible day of school, walking through the halls, knowing Daddy was gone and not able to say a thing to anyone. It didn't matter. It didn't change a thing. But it was what I had wanted to hear for thirty years. For just a moment, I was glad she had lived to say those words.

"None of you knew how hard things got after Daddy was gone," she added.

I sat up straighter, ready to hear things I wanted to know for so many years.

"We very nearly lost the farm. None of our suppliers wanted to give me credit. None of them thought I could make a go of this business by myself. I wasn't sure I could do it alone either. But I had to try. I had three lovely children to care for and to educate. Daddy wanted you all to have the opportunities we never had. So, I kept trying. I had your dad's brother, Uncle Ralph who worked with me and George, of course. He worked for us for nearly forty years, until he passed.

"I was just about to my last dollar when Mr. Orlando offered to give me a line of credit to buy the supplies I needed for spring. We had a good crop that year and I paid it back. Each year, he extended the line of credit a little more, and we expanded. I built the apple store because I had trouble selling my produce. We made more money than ever. Not one of those suppliers ever said they were sorry, but they all came with their hands out ready to take my money when we were well on our feet again."

She paused for a bit, then got a sly, wicked smile I had never seen before and continued.

"I never gave them a dime. I bought everything from Mr. Orlando. It was so much fun telling them 'No.' I'd always say, 'Try me again next year,' just so I could have the pleasure of saying no again."

She laughed for the first time in a very long time. We both laughed.

The story took a lot out of Mom and she soon fell asleep. I sat watching her like I had never seen her before.

I was sixteen when my father died. I was old enough that I should have known these things, but I must have been too wrapped up in teenage stuff to notice. Back then, I noticed when she missed my basketball games and when I had to make dinner so many times. I knew she was working hard. I knew sometimes she cried at night. But, so did I. I didn't think about how this was on her. I had too much bottled-up grief to think of anyone else. I did know, though, that she drove 150 miles just to have lunch with me on parent's day at college, then drove back again to close the store. I couldn't imagine what it took to do that. I don't think I could have done it.

Three o'clock came quickly. It was time for our meeting. The social worker's office was on the first floor of the hospital. She had a neat little office with a pleasant sitting area. I met Maria and John there. I noticed how the room was designed to be soothing: soft green walls, comfortable chairs, and just a touch of flowered wall paper. There were signs that this was a Christian hospital too: framed Bible passages, an ornamental cross, and a picture of Jesus welcoming someone to heaven. This must all be carefully calculated to comfort the grieving, I guess. Then I wondered if I was to be one of the grieving.

"My name is Nancy," the pleasant lady said after we were seated. "We need to talk about your mother's care when she leaves the hospital."

Such a pleasant voice for such ugly words, I thought.

"We don't want to go back to the Garden House," John snapped. "Mom didn't like that much."

"The Garden House is for rehab," Nancy said pleasantly. "Your mother will need skilled nursing care at this point. The doctor doesn't think she will be able to tolerate much therapy."

"We would like to be able to keep her home," Maria said. "She hates to be away from home."

"I understand," the nurse replied. "But she will need twenty-four-hour care. Her medications now are very complicated. She needs monitoring and blood work on a regular basis. She will need assistance getting to the bathroom. Bathing will be complicated. She won't be able to prepare meals or care for herself. Do you have long-term healthcare for your mom?"

"Yes, but she doesn't want that," Maria said, near tears. "Isn't there some way we can care for her at home?"

"You could a get a full-time nurse, but it's very expensive. Even if the nurse just comes every other day, it's awfully expensive, but it's your choice. And you should think about who will be there at night."

"I could move in with her," John offered. "I could just check on my house from time to time. There's room for me."

"Here are some brochures," Nancy said. "Please take a look. I understand your mother has had a stroke. Sometimes, stroke patients do improve. Your mother might benefit from a month or so of full-time care, then if she improves, you could take her home. The decision is up to you, but I do think, at this point, a skilled nursing facility is best. Taking care of someone in this situation is very difficult. I'll give you some time to discuss your options. Please stay as long as you like. But you should know that your mom can only stay in the hospital two more days. She must move somewhere else by Sunday."

Nancy left and we sat in silence. No pressure. Just make one of the most important decisions in your life in two days. We had had this discussion several times. Our opinions weren't going to change, although the urgency was different. Maria and John both knew where I stood. I didn't want to start the argument again. But some things had changed. Mom was less mobile, and I had—well, I didn't know yet what I had.

"We could take shifts," John started. "Let's say I stayed Sunday, Monday; and Carrie stayed Wednesday and Thursday; and Maria—"

I knew it was time to put my messy cards on the table.

Before John could finish, I spoke, "I can't next Thursday. I'm not sure I can for some time. I'm having a procedure next Thursday to remove a growth from my uterus. I won't know until after the procedure what that means and if there will be more treatment."

"Oh, Carrie, why didn't you tell us?" Maria cried. "Is it—is it cancer?"

"I don't know. The doctor doesn't think so but it could be."

Now I was having trouble holding back the tears.

"John," Maria said softly, "this changes things. It will be really hard to care for Mom without Carrie's help, and she may need our help too. I think we should try the nursing home, if only for a while. When Carrie is back on her feet, we can bring Mom home. I think we all need some time before we are caring full time for Mom. It won't be forever."

John agreed and we opened the brochures. We spent the next two days visiting nursing homes and asking questions. None of them were great. All of them were a lot of money.

Everything about the nursing home was scary. The food looked dreadful. The furnishings were dreary. The staff was indifferent. The cost was astronomical. Finally, we found one that was very well located, an easy drive for all of us, and it had lovely fountains and gardens. It was well kept and the staff we met were pleasant. We made arrangements for Mom to move in on Sunday. I offered to handle the transfer, as before, partly because I didn't know how long I'd be able to help.

This time things were different. Mom did not object so much, mostly because she was too weak to object much. She was preregistered so the checking-in process was easier. We got to her room quickly and a nurse came soon after we arrived to get her settled.

"I'm not staying long," Mom told the nurse. "They don't want me home yet, but I'll just be here a little while and then I can go home."

The nurse smiled and I cried. Home! Again with going home. It's always home. I can't understand how or why it has such a powerful draw. Here is my mother who can't do a thing for herself, but still she wants to be at that blasted house. It's taken every spare minute we have to keep the place from falling apart, but she wants to be there. Sometimes I wonder if she cares at all how much it takes for us to take care of her home. Does she know how much we have to sacrifice to care for her there? Why does she cling so hard to that damn, dirty house? Why isn't this nice, clean place enough?

My mind was racing while I watched the nurse and the orderly setting up the room and putting Mom's things away. I wondered if she would leave this place. I wondered how often I'd be able to come and talk with her.

As soon as they left, Mom gave me directions on rearranging everything. I made sure she had her comb, tissues, and toothbrush in reach. I suggested we watch TV, but Mom would have none of that. She never enjoyed TV as much as most of my generation did. Maybe that's why the loss of mobility was so hard. Myself, I think I'd be happy to have the opportunity to watch TV all day. I'd be good at it. Maybe it's the fact that she can't do anything else that makes it so hard.

Soon it was time for dinner. I wheeled Mom into the cheerful dining room and sat next to her. The administrator said I could eat with her today. Dinner was roasted chicken and mashed potatoes with steamed veggies and Jell-O. It didn't have much flavor, but it wasn't bad.

Mom ate well. I asked her how it was and she said, "Terrible."

"Oh, Mom, it's not that bad," I retorted.

"Almost Inedible" she snorted, cleaning her plate.

I just sighed and wheeled her back to her room. I tucked her into bed and kissed her good night.

As I walked to my car, I knew this wasn't going to be easy. Nothing with Mom is ever easy. Maybe that's just the way God designed it. Maybe it's payback for raising us. I'm sure there were times when she thought, *Nothing with those kids is ever easy.*

I needed to go home and hug somebody. Geoff was glad. Adam was puzzled. I just told him, "You'll get it someday." He was good with that.

I spent a lot of time with Mom over the next three days. I knew it would be much harder after whatever was going to happen on Thursday, so I wanted to give Maria and John a break. I went in the morning to see she if she had had her breakfast and sometimes went again in the afternoon. In between I was tying down loose ends at work. I wanted to make sure my clients would not need everything while I was out.

I called each of them and told them I'd be out for about a week on personal business. I didn't feel good about the little lie, but everybody said it was bad business to tell them I was sick. Since I *was* my business, clients might start looking for alternatives if they think I might have to close. I was sure none of my clients would do that, but business is business. You can only expect so much from clients, and mine had been very understanding. In any case, they were three very long days and the busier I was the less I thought about the future.

Chapter 17
Side Stepping the Big C

Finally, Thursday came. Geoff and I were at the hospital at six sharp. I had gotten up before five o'clock and sat and prayed for a while. I asked God to guide the doctors today as they operated. I asked Him to watch over my family and keep us strong, no matter what happened. I woke Adam to say goodbye, which only confused him more. Geoff was in a very good mood, or so it seemed, and I found that annoying. I was so scared; I was nearly shaking.

St. Mark's had very comfortable same-day surgery pre-op rooms. They were just big enough for a big, comfy lounge chair and one extra chair. I quickly got changed into a hospital gown and handed off my clothes to the nurse. She took blood and we filled out forms. She explained that there may be a need for a full hysterectomy. I signed papers allowing them to do that. I wanted to pull the paper back and say, *No,* but I didn't.

Geoff and I talked and joked around. He was great at keeping the conversation light. The nurse came back and put in an IV. Finally, it was time to be carted off to surgery. Geoff gave me a kiss and big smile as they wheeled me away.

I was cold. Something inside of me was screaming, *Don't go. Don't let them do this,* but it was too late. I recited the Lord's Prayer in my head. The nurse took my glasses, so I was blind too. Everything was a blur. It's amazing how strange things look from the prone angle. Even though I had been through these halls many times with Mom, I couldn't quite recognize where we were going. Then we were in the OR. It was very cold and bright. I tried to say the 23 Psalm but kept forgetting parts. I prayed again. There were so many people milling about. I seemed so confused.

I heard my doctor say, "Good morning, Mrs. Young. This is Dr. Hughes. Did the nurse explain that we may have to do a hysterectomy?"

"Yes," I replied weakly. The monster inside of me was screaming, *No, stop him.*

"That's good," said Dr. Hughes.

No, it's not good! I wanted to scream. None of this is good. But I was getting sleepy. I tried to pray again, but my mind couldn't focus. I heard the doctor tell the nurse something, "Get the..." what, I don't remember. They were talking, but it wasn't making any sense. Then everything was still. The room got dark and quiet. I was flying, don't know where, just floating above the clouds. It was all quite pleasant.

Then there were voices again, muffled voices. I was very sleepy but trying to make out what they were saying. Someone said, "Your operation is over, Mrs. Young. You are in recovery."

Operation? What operation? Where was I?

The room was coming into focus. My mouth was very, very dry. I wanted to say something, but nothing was coming out. Little by little, it was coming back to me. I had had surgery, something about a growth. It all happened so quickly. Surely, I was only asleep for second.

"Mrs. Young, can you take a drink?" the nurse said.

I didn't want to drink. I just wanted to sleep. I wish they would just let me go to sleep.

"Just take a sip," she said again.

I sipped. It felt good in my parched throat, but not good enough to make the effort.

There seemed to be a lot of noise now. There were tubes here and there. Nothing felt quite right. There was pain. Too much pain. I needed to go back to sleep. If I could just go back to flying, everything would be okay.

"We're going to let your husband in," said one of the nurses. "Is that okay? I think he's anxious to see you."

I nodded. I think I nodded. The room was getting clearer. I was remembering. I had surgery. I had a growth. I wondered how it went. I knew I didn't have this pain when I came to the hospital. I wondered what time of day it was. Then Geoff was there.

"How are you feeling?" he asked gently.

"I'm pretty foggy. I'm having trouble putting everything together."

"The surgery went well," he told me. "They did a hysterectomy, but you're going to be fine."

Now I was remembering everything.

"It can't be all that great," I said, a little too sarcastically. "They did the hysterectomy."

"That was more of a precaution," Geoff offered. "The growth, was probably benign, but it may be precancerous. The doctor said this will keep it from coming back and getting worse. You'll be up and about in no time."

"I bet I can't go dancing tonight?" I retorted. "Sorry," I quickly added, "must be the drugs."

Geoff was smiling. That was a good sign.

Soon the nurse was back, yanking at things and talking about going to a room. It wasn't my plan to stay in the hospital tonight. It wasn't my plan to have this growth or this hysterectomy. I'm not sure it was even God's plan. It just was. And it hurt.

It was noon when the nurse wheeled me into my room. I was fully awake and fully aware of the pain, terrible pain. The nurse brought more drugs and it helped. Geoff looked very bored as I went in and out of consciousness. In one of my awake periods, I told him to go to work. He was glad of that. The nurse brought lunch. I took one look and vomited all over everything. It was so embarrassing.

I was asleep again. It was a great sleep with no pain and flying again. Then I was awake and Maria was there. The pain was terrible. Maria found a nurse for me and more pain medication. She also found some Jell-O for me to eat and helped me find my mouth. She talked about fond memories of childhood. It was great to have her there. She made me comfortable and helped me forget about the pain. She ordered me a nice supper and stayed to help me eat it. We talked about our kids and our husbands. We laughed and we cried. She made the time pass so quickly.

It was nearly dark when she left. I thanked God for a successful operation and for my sister. I'm not sure I ever realized how lucky I am to have a sister. I'm sure I never appreciated her more.

I left the hospital the next day, sore and woozy, but a little better. At home I mostly slept. Two days later, the doctor called and told me the cyst was benign. No more treatment. No chemo. I was going to be okay, but I'd be going through menopause now. Yea. Time to celebrate, I think.

I got stronger each day and, in a week, I was back at work and "Mom duty." I never told Mom any of this, of course. We weren't very good at sharing things, and I was sure she wouldn't understand.

Before I was completely back, Maria and John had taken Mom home. They hired a part-time nurse to help. This nurse grew up on a farm and understood Mom much better.

She has been saying for some time that it was her wish to die in her own home. I didn't think she really understood the ramifications of that wish for her children, but we had to listen to her. After all she had listened to and provided for so many of our wishes, some of which we would never know her personal cost.

While I got stronger, Mom got weaker and more confused. One Sunday when I came to see her, she told me a long story of how a doctor came to her house in the middle of the night and operated on her hurting knee. She was so sure this happened she asked me to find the bloody rags he left. I took her all over the house looking for signs of surgery and found nothing. But she just said, "He cleaned it all up very well."

Sometimes she talked to her parents and sometimes to my dad. Clearly, she was slipping closer and closer to the end. The day came when her doctor recommended hospice. It was another difficult family meeting.

We had an informative and scary meeting with a hospice representative. After she left, we discussed the options. John, to no one's surprise, was dead set against hospice.

"You want Mom to die," he said.

"No, of course I don't want Mom to die," I retorted. "But I don't want her to live in pain either."

"I know this is selfish," Maria said softly, "but I'm just not ready to say goodbye."

"The hospice lady never said this was an immediate end or that they would in any way hasten the end," I just couldn't see their perspective.

"You do know there is a very clear reason why the doctor recommended hospice, don't you?" I asked. "He has seen something that signals Mom will not recover. Hospice means pain relief for Mom and help for us. Look at all the things they provide, at no cost," I nearly shouted, waving the brochure.

"No," John said emphatically. "They said she can't get any medical intervention that would prolong her life. What if she had something like the gallbladder thing. She couldn't get that operation."

"She can get any treatment that would ease pain. I think the gallbladder operation would apply. Look, if she did need something that doesn't qualify under hospice, we can exit hospice and come back to it later. I don't want to lose her either, but I also don't want to see her in pain. I know where she's going. We know what joy and peace she will have in heaven."

"Why did Dr. Schultz recommend hospice?" Maria asked. "Did he tell anyone?"

"He may have told the hospice people, but they can't talk about it," I answered.

"Well, first we need all the information," Maria added. "Then we'll make the decision."

Maria called Dr. Schultz immediately. A few minutes later he called back. She said "Okay. Thanks," and hung up.

Face grim, Maria said, "Dr. Schultz said Mom's heart is failing." She could hardly get the words out. "It can't be too long. He recommended hospice, so we could keep her home and keep her comfortable."

We both looked at John. After a few minutes, he said, "Okay. I suppose it's time. But if I don't like the way they treat her, we're out. Agreed?"

We both said yes. What else could we say?

It was a very hard meeting, but we were so cried-out we had no more tears. Just resolve to make these last months, weeks, days, the best they could be.

Within twenty-four hours of signing the papers, hospice had given Mom a new hospital bed, new bedside commode, new wheelchair, and walker. Everything that was possibly needed to keep her in her home just showed up on the doorstep. They provided adult diapers and medical equipment, and best of all, a kind, loving nurse who came every other day.

John had moved into the house, and he was there most of the time. I came every third day and slept over if John had to go home. We all got to be good friends with the hospice nurse, Sarah. She was our angel, guiding us through a troubled storm.

We called Mom's siblings and they all came to say goodbye. Now each day was a gift. We cherished these last days. She was seldom awake, probably from the morphine. When she was awake, we gave her ice cream and held her hand. We each, in turn, told her we loved her and would miss her, but knew she would be with Jesus. We read the Bible. Pastor Mueller came and prayed with her and with us.

Finally, the day came, the hospice nurse said she thought tomorrow would probably be Mom's last day. I went home, knowing I wouldn't sleep. I couldn't touch any of my dinner. Geoff was so sweet and understanding, but I really didn't want anybody to comfort me. I just wanted to talk with God.

I finally fell asleep around midnight and woke up suddenly at five a.m. I woke with a poem about Mom in my head. I ran to my office and put the poem to paper. Then I showered and changed and left for Mom's house. Maria, of course, wanted to make some changes to the poem. Loved it, but still wanted to make changes. Changes that, much to my annoyance, made it better. That's Maria.

It was one of the longest days of my life. Around two p.m. Uncle Fred came. He said he wanted to talk with Mom alone. He went in the room and came out about fifteen minutes later. He said nothing but went straight to his car and left.

Ten minutes later our precious mother passed from this world to heaven. I was standing at the end of her bed. Maria on my right and John on my left. Right in the middle again. I thought I felt a swift breeze float pass me and Maria said, "She's gone."

The nurse came in and confirmed Maria's pronouncement. Our mother was in heaven. I thought I could see the huge smile on Daddy's face as he welcomed her in. Together again.

The next few days were a blur. Julie came home as did all Maria's family. Pastor Mueller led a beautiful service ending at the cemetery where Mom was laid to rest next to Daddy, as it should be. We cried. We hugged. We toasted Mom and remembered. I remember very little of it. Mom was with us no more.

At the service, on the back of the bulletin was my poem:

My Mother

Did you know my mother?
Did you know her well?
Maybe you saw the old lady, bent with age
Maybe you saw the endless smile
Beneath the snow white hair
Maybe you saw her gentleness
From a kind old sage

Did you know my mother?
She was once a child
In a large happy family
Working hard on a farm
Brothers, and sisters she held so dear
Picking strawberries together
They grew through the years.

Did you know my mother?
She was once a bride
Leaving her family so young
For a man once despised
With little money, but hearts full of love
They worked hard together
Trusting in God above.

Did you know my mother?
She once chased her toddlers
In a small three-room house
Side-by-side with her husband
They grew orchards and plants
Building family and business
With a prayer and some chance.

Did you know my mother?
The hardships she bore?
Losing her husband with children to raise
To care for her family
The orchard business she saved
Working hard day and night
She never complained.

Did you know my mother?
Her unshaken faith?
No matter the challenge
God was her strength
Her passion to brighten,
God's house with flowers
Was the mission she left us
With her faith in our Savior

Did you know my mother?
She lived to give love
She gave to her children, selfless and willing
She gave her God, service fulfilling
Even crippled and sick, shé was always giving
To be just like her
Is a life worth our living

On the first anniversary of Mom's passing, Maria, John, and I met at the cemetery. We brought our folding yard chairs and a bottle of wine. We toasted Mom and Dad and reminisced. It was a beautiful fall evening. I felt more at peace than I had in a long time. My business was going to be okay. I was going to be okay. Our parents were together in heaven. They were okay.

I realized that this long arduous journey of Mom's last years was not a trial from God, but a gift. A glorious gift. That's the way with gifts from God. We never really see them as gifts at the time. We may even rail against them or throw Bibles—hopefully not the Bibles. But during this time, I had learned more about my mother than I had in my previous forty years.

God gave me the chance to get to know her. Really know her, love her, and appreciate her. He taught me patience and understanding. He taught me to recognize the things that are truly important. He taught me to trust Him. And I think he was preparing me for my future. For we don't know our future. Only He knows. God is good. All the time.

The end

Epilogue

It's been eight years now since my mother passed away. I think with all major events like this, it takes some time to see the actual impact. When I look back, all the struggle and all the anxiety of that period seems to melt away. I'm left only with the overwhelming joy and gratitude to God for the time I had, one-on-one, with my mother. Time that I might never have had had she passed away during that first scary hospital visit.

Although I talk to God all the time, I'm still learning to listen to him. I'm not sure of all his plans for me, but I know there were lessons from this period that I was meant to learn. Some, I'm still learning.

Since Mom died, my business has progressed well. I won't be on any top list of anything, but, that's okay. My business has helped provide enough to put Adam through four years of business school—Praise God, he graduated! And it paid for a lovely wedding for Julie and Paul. My kids are well and working in jobs with benefits. Isn't that all any parent can hope for?

I'm doing well. Aging, and with that comes the usual annoying little issues, but I really can't complain—oh, I could, but shouldn't. Geoff is still working, too, but planning for retirement in the not-too-distant future. I'm sure that will bring all sorts of new challenges, which we will face.

However, the biggest change in my life is that I am now caregiver for Uncle Fred. Even before Mom passed, I had started to look after Uncle Fred. He sold his farm in the country about five years before Mom passed and moved into a little house that just happened to be a couple of miles from me. Since he never married, we were his only family. Sure, there were others, most of them had been closer to Uncle

Fred than me, but they were now either in the country or otherwise unable to spend much time with him. I was nearly next door, and with my new company I had plenty of flexibility to help out.

He spent all his holidays with us. I made him meals once or twice a week and started taking him to his doctor appointments. At one visit, something told me I should go in with him. Uncle Fred was talking about a problem he had—I really, really didn't want to hear that—and the doctor said, "Now, Fred, we've talked about this. You have Parkinson's Disease. Some of these things are a result of this disease. Are you taking all of you medications?"

To this Uncle Fred said, "I don't ever recall talking about any Parkinson's. I take most of the medications, most of the time, I think."

The doctor gave me one of those looks that says, *Aren't you the caregiver? Then give him some care.*

When I found my voice, I said, "I'll make sure my uncle takes his medicine."

From that day on, I have taken care of Uncle Fred. I got pill boxes and filled them weekly. I went to his house nearly every other day to make sure he was taking them and checking that he was eating and taking care of himself.

As his mobility and memory continued to fail, we talked about a nursing home. Unlike my mother, Uncle Fred liked the idea of a nursing home. We visited a few and found one we both liked. It was close enough I could visit often and had multiple options for continued care. And, most importantly, the food was good.

Uncle Fred settled in quickly. He goes to Bible study, exercise class, and the frequent music programs. He plays bingo—although he complained about that silly game—and paints. My rugged farmer uncle paints! I try to visit three times week.

We don't have much in common, but he loves to play dominos, and I'm getting pretty good. As his memory fails, he doesn't always recognize me, but he can still beat me at bingo.

I'm the executor of his estate, which means I pay all the bills, do his taxes, argue with the insurance company when required, and make sure he has enough to pay the nursing home. I check in with the nurses a couple times a week and go to all the care-planning meetings. I make sure there's a cake for his birthday and holiday decorations. It's a lot. But I've been well trained.

Yes, there are times when I feel like I've had enough. I don't often know what God is saying, but this I'm certain: God gave me the job of taking care of Uncle Fred and I'll see it to the end. Maybe, just maybe, the trials of taking care of Mom prepared me for this task.

I'm standing again in the cemetery, visiting Mom. I've come here today to pick out a plot for Uncle Fred. I feel God will soon call him home. I've made all the plans, so it won't be so hard when the time comes, as it surely must. Uncle Fred wants to be laid to rest next to two of his sisters who are buried in this cemetery. Someday, I, too, will rest here, or at least my remains will. I know where I'll be.

I recall years ago one of my father's sisters made me a lovely needle point. It's a piece of art really. The picture is an intricate bouquet of flowers of many different kinds and colors in a striking orange vase. Beautiful. However, if you turn it over all you see is a wild mess of yarn going here and there with no apparent rhyme or reason. You would never guess that that ugly pile of yarn could make such a lovely picture. I think that's how life is. While we often see only all the mess, God sees the beautiful picture. And, someday, I believe I will be able to see it too.

But for now, I will prepare for whatever comes next. I think that will be something very wonderful.

Julie just told me she's expecting a baby. I'm going to be a grandma. What a wonderful adventure lies ahead. God is good. All the time.

About the Author

Carin Fahr Shulusky was born and raised in west St. Louis County with her siblings, Mary, Linda and Larry. Her parents owned a greenhouse business providing cut flowers to local florists. She was always interested in writing. She won a poetry competition in 8th grade and was editor of her high school (Lafayette High) newspaper. Carin attended the University of Missouri, Columbia, where she received a B.J (Bachelor of Journalism '73). After college she worked in advertising for GE Plastics where she was the first professional woman in that division and then for Monsanto's Agricultural Division where she was the first professional woman in their corporate headquarters.

After 25 years in Marketing, she created her own firm, Marketing Alliance. She was president of Marketing Alliance, from 2002 – 2014. She is a past-president of the Business Marketing Association of St. Louis and has received their Lifetime Achievement Award. She was a member of the National Association of Press Women. Carin serves on the board of the Special Education Foundation. She is a volunteer for Springboard to Learning as a coach with their WiseWrite program.

Carin Fahr married Richard Shulusky in 1975. They have two children; Christine Shulusky Blonn and Andrew Shulusky. They are proud grandparents to the marvelous Sophie Blonn. Grandma Carin has a life long love of cooking, even writing her own cookbook.

Carin is a voracious reader. She loves Jane Austin, Harry Potter and Elizabeth Peters among many, many others. In addition to the cookbook, she's written poetry and children's stories, as yet unpublished. Carin retired in 2014 to devote full time to writing. Her first book, *In the*

Middle was inspired by her own battle to care for her beloved mother, Dorothy Hoehne Fahr. Many of the stories Carrie Young's mother tells her in *In the Middle* came from Carin's mother.

Carin is a lifelong member of, Pathfinder Church in Ellisville, Missouri. She has long been involved in her church, including 40 years of teaching Sunday school and VBS. She served on short term missions to Belize ten times. Carin also tutored at a magnet school in the College Hill neighborhood of North St. Louis for five years.

You may contact Carin at carinshulusky.com or follow her on Facebook or Instagram or Twitter.